CONCRETE WINGS

CONCRETE WINGS

One Man's Fifty Year Journey To Personal Freedom

Beverly Gandara

CONCRETE WINGS

ISBN: 978-0-9971406-0-6

Disclaimer: *This book is the sole expression and opinion of its author. Names, characters, business organizations, places, events and incidents are the product of the author and used fictitiously to protect those who may still be living. No warranties or guarantees are expressed or implied by the author's choice to include any of the content in this volume. The author shall not be liable for any physical, psychological, emotional, financial, or commercial damages, including, but not limited to, special, incidental, consequential or other damages. The views and rights are the same: you the reader are responsible for your own choices.*

Printed in the United States of America

First Edition – V2.3

Published by
Burlibooks, LLC
Burlington, Wisconsin

ACKNOWLEDGEMENT

Much of the information about the political climate in Cuba while Julian was growing up comes directly from his parents and their memories over the years, and through the opinions of relatives and neighbors.

ADDITIONAL INFORMATION:

Wikipedia contributors, "The History of Cuba," Wikipedia, the Free Encyclopedia: https//en.wikipedia.org/history of Cuba. (Accessed September 14, 2015.)

Wikipedia contributors, "Bay of Pigs Invasion," Wikipedia, The Free Encyclopedia: https//en.wikipedia.org/wiki/bay of pigs invasion. (Accessed September 21, 2015.)

www.historyofcuba.com written and compiled by J. A. Sierra

Cover artwork
"The Returning" by Brian Boner

Cover design
by Armand Gandara & Bruce Feigenbaum

Back cover photo of Beverly Gandara
by George Atoraya Simonov

CONCRETE WINGS

DEDICATION

For Armand, simply the love of my life. I am privileged to share his journey. I am blessed by his unconditional love and forever grateful for his intelligence, strength and beauty—inside and out.

For Tony DeMarco, for his kindness, and generosity with his time, knowledge and support, with sincere appreciation and gratitude.

For Honora Levin, a dear friend and fine writer for her generosity in setting an easy path to follow.

PROLOGUE

September, 2015
Delray Beach, Florida

Dear Reader:

This book is fiction inspired by a story told to me over a period of several years. Raised by a quiet but powerful chauvinistic man, a gorgeous undiagnosed dyslexic with an uncontrollable temper, and ruled by a dictator with communistic leanings, there was little chance for personal growth and independent thought in Havana, Cuba in the nineteen fifties.

As a naïve teen, Julian was sent out of Cuba on the eve of the Bay of Pigs Invasion to save smuggled family jewels, avoid the draft into Castro's army, and anchor his family in America. Coming of age in New York at the height of the sexual revolution, he gained the freedom he sought. By a twist of fate, he began to lose his freedom when his oppressive parents arrived, refused to assimilate into American society, and treated him as if he was still a child.

Torn between protecting family secrets and traditions, while he strived for the American Dream, Julian was dissuaded from seeking an education and a career. After two failed relationships and a series of go nowhere jobs, he finally met the love of his life. Together they turned a hobby into a business and eventually moved to Arizona where he made peace with the ghosts of his past, and found comfort in the extraordinary beauty of the desert. An improved quality of life allowed him to care for his elderly parents with the love and respect they deserved, until their passing. In the end, Julian learns that success isn't always based on what one becomes; often it is measured by what one overcomes

Originally written as a screenplay, I wove Julian's fifty year journey to freedom into one hundred-twenty pages, which placed in a couple of contests, but that gave me little room to flesh out many details, and to add the humor which kept this compelling story fluid and fascinating.

I hope you enjoy reading this story.

Beverly Gandara.

BOOK I

Havana, Cuba

CHAPTER ONE

June, 1950
Havana, Cuba

My name is Julian Vida. My parents, Anita and Arturo Vida, are gone now. While I loved them dearly, I was often torn by my respect for them and for their ancestral traditions, their secrets that I kept, and my pride in becoming an American citizen. My earliest memories begin with "special" weekends with my mother. One particular Saturday is forever imprinted on my memory. Confused and frightened, I was happy and sad at the same time. It was my introduction to what would become a painful secret which I kept for decades. I was five years old.

Anita, my mother, thirty-three, a functioning voluptuary, had long thick blond hair, porcelain skin, and a seductive charm she used to flirt through life. At five foot three she had a curvy figure of which she was quite proud, and never missed an opportunity to reveal it in public through her manner of dress and in her measured physical movements, like walking—no rather swaying, and by sitting in posed position ever aware of her silhouette. It was as if she lived in front of a mirror when she was out of the house. Inside the house, she was an obedient wife and attentive mother; both roles tainted with the dark secrets of her erratic behavior. Anita was in complete and sole control of everything concerning me. She kept me clean, well-groomed and fed. To keep me busy, she took me grocery shopping every day to purchase fresh food for our meals. Often, she took me to Woolworth's for toys, particularly plane and ship models, and puzzles and books—to keep me busy inside the house where she could keep a smothering eye on me. I had a childhood devoid of friends, sports, physical or outside activities.

My father, Arturo was about thirty-seven at the time. He was handsome, muscular, strong-willed and confident, and focused with a smooth manner. He was an emotional withholder who never raised his voice, but his piercing eyes told you exactly where you stood at any moment. Everyone who knew him feared *the silent stare*. Arturo was a voracious reader who lived by a self-imposed code of behavior, and used his energy minimally. He was simply a powerful man. He maintained a strict routine in our house, to which my mother and I complied. We arose every day at six, ate breakfast at seven, lunch at noon, dinner by six and retired for the night at nine sharp. Arturo loved two things in life: his money and my mother. And he dearly loved my mother.

"Julian, tomorrow is a special day," my mother said.

That promised a happy surprise with lots of candy and soda; my little mind was filled with an imaginary party with friends with whom I could play. I hardly slept the night before in anticipation of the glorious Saturday. I was well-groomed in white shorts and a crisp white shirt. I skipped alongside Anita, lavishly bejeweled, heavily made-up and coiffed in a flowing white print dress, and smelling of lavender, her favorite scent. She wore white gloves and a sun hat over her long blonde hair. She was beautiful and she knew it.

As we walked the wavy, cobblestoned streets, Perez Prado's musical version of the "Peanut Vendor" by Moisés Simons wafted through the open doors and windows of the slim two-story buildings. Big, shiny, American cars wound their way through the narrow streets, horns blaring. Because of the steamy hot weather, doors and windows were open to take advantage of the soft tropical ocean breeze. Music filled the air as did the pleasant odor of café con leche (fresh coffee brewed with steamed milk). It was a common beverage for all Cubans. In fact, I have been drinking today's café latte since I was a child. Everything smelled good. The sun shone brightly, the music was pleasant, and Anita's firm hand was about to lead me to a highly anticipated adventure. It started out as a glorious day.

Laughter and gentle teasing filled the streets as women shoppers in white gloves, sun hats, flowing skirts and ruffled blouses were flirted with by men loitering outside small businesses smoking cigars. The men wore straw hats and white shirts meant to be worn outside their light-colored slacks. As we crossed through the park, the peanut vendor wolf-whistled at my mother. She sauntered over with me in tow. I was mesmerized when he took a brown piece of paper, eight and a half by eleven and like magic shaped it into a cone and filled it with hot shelled peanuts which he had roasted in a tin box the size of a suitcase. He pinched the end, and handed it to me with a flourish. Immediately I unwrapped it and popped the hot peanuts into my mouth. They were delicious! Anita handed the vendor five centavos, the equivalent of five pennies. He folded the money back into her hand and said, "The pleasure of seeing your beauty is payment enough for me."

"Well, if you insist," my mother purred while putting the money away.

As we walked away I turned to look at the vendor and watched as he ogled my mother's body. Uncomfortable, I started to skip to distract him. Smack! She hit me on the head.

"Walk straight!"

We continued our stroll past a flower shop and the florist stepped outside to hand my mother a red rose and sneered.

"Hey Blondie, what sensational hips. Have my first born."

"What does that mean, Mama?"

Thwap! My mother slapped me on the head, twirled her hair and accelerated her wiggle.

"He's speaking to me. You don't speak until you are spoken to!"

"I'm sorry, Mama. Please don't hit me again."

Whack! "You're talking again."

I learned early to swallow my tears and keep my head down. I still didn't know where we were going. It was hot and noisy and by then I just wanted to go home to my room and my toys, who were my only friends. Suddenly, my mother stopped. She yanked me to a stop as well. We were standing in front of the local movie theater.

I recognized Rafael, a waxed mustached policeman. He was tall, broad and physically fit. He moved like an animal circling his prey, constantly checking his surroundings. He must have been on a break because he was still focused on my mother as he leaned on a 1950 Chevrolet. The car windows were open. He reached in and turned on the radio to Nat King Cole singing "Mona Lisa." My mother's coquettishness was exaggerated as she rushed toward him. I skipped alongside her, thinking it was a game. I stopped abruptly as they kissed. Rafael lifted me in the air, settled me back on earth and made believe he was boxing with me as he did so many times in my home. He was my father's friend.

. . .

Rafael and my mother laughed as we all went into the theater together. I was still uneasy, but my mother was having such a good time I thought maybe we were playing a game and it was okay. I sat quietly alone in the theater, my hands filled with candy and soda. My mother and Rafael sat two rows behind me. I turned around and saw Rafael kiss and fondle my mother, and I knew that was wrong. I tried to watch the cartoons while listening to the other children giggle. There was no party and no one to play with. Tears began falling from my eyes.

As we exited the theater, I watched a man and woman approach the Chevrolet Rafael had leaned on when we first arrived. The man removed a ticket from the windshield. He looked around and reached in to turn off the radio then he opened the door for the woman. He eyed Rafael and made a fast getaway. Rafael, the policeman, had done his job for the day. Rafael kissed my mother and said to her,

"Make sure the kid don't talk."

"Don't worry, he won't," she responded.

Rafael waved and left. My mother watched after him. I whimpered. She kneeled next me, wiped my tears and then slapped my face.

"I told you, no crying."

"Why did you kiss Rafael?" I asked between sobs.

She leaned closer.

"It's our secret, if you want to see cartoons every week you have to promise never to tell Papa that Rafael comes with us."

"But why Mama, why can't Papa come with us to the movies?"

She stiffened.

"Your Papa is a very important businessman. He has no time for you. If you tell him, Rafael will have to shoot him dead and it will all be your fault."

I didn't say another word—for decades

We returned home in silence. I refused to speak to my mother, so instead I focused on the stores lining our block. The bodega was on the corner and normally we would have stopped in to purchase groceries for the day. We drifted past the lighting store, the furniture store, the barber shop and the apartment building, the newspaper office across the street, the watch repair store and the coffee shop were bristling with energy. People were walking about and in and out of the stores and apartments above or behind them. I looked up. The Spanish Colonial buildings to me were giants. Many of them were like my father's building where he had his antique store on the street level and the seven room townhouse we lived in upstairs. He lingered in the doorway of his store unaware we were about to approach.

Dressed in the typical Cuban long-sleeve white shirt, called a guyabera, which had two rows of stitches down the front and that he wore over his black slacks, he chewed on his freshly rolled cigar. His frisbee-sized eyes glistened as a sexy teenage girl passed him by and captured his attention.

"Your breeze as you pass me kisses my cheek. May I kiss you back?" he inquired. She giggled and moved on.

As we came up behind him, my mother yelled.

"In front of my house?"

My father, unruffled, said softly, "Your house? Go upstairs and take your son with you."

I grabbed his leg and looked up at him with reverence.

"Papa, I have peanuts. Do you want some?"

He just looked down at me and mocked me.

"I have peanuts!"

He shook me from his leg and I fell onto the sidewalk. My peanuts scattered into the gutter. My mother yanked me up and smacked me on the head.

"You dirtied your pants, get upstairs!"

My father quietly demanded of my mother, "Clean up that mess and get upstairs. I want dinner on the table at six sharp. I'm going back to work."

Bam! Bam! She punched me right across my back.

In a shrill voice, she screamed.

"That's twice, once for making a mess and twice for embarrassing me in public!"

Just then, I saw my neighbor Mara the hairdresser and her son Angelo approach; he was three years older. I was happy to see them, maybe the hitting would stop and I could play with Angelo. My mother had her hair washed and styled every week by Mara and of course I had to accompany her. So sometimes under the careful eye of my mother, I was allowed to play with Angelo by the sinks at the back of the beauty parlor. He taught me checkers and marbles and often talked about dying. I received my first lesson in humiliation when I heard Angelo inquire, "Why does Mrs. Vida hit Julian so much?"

Mara covered Angelo's eyes, turned and led him away and said, "Her heavy hand is none of our business."

"But I want to play with Julian,"

"She'll be in next week," Mara said.

Later that night, frightened by the day's events and ignored by both my parents, I couldn't sleep so I left my little room filled with French antique furniture and toys to go to my parents' room.

We shared a common wall. Anita and Arturo never realized that I heard everything they said, and remembered so much even if I didn't understand it at the time. Over the years, my parents graciously and with startling honesty answered most of my questions. I needed a hug but I heard them talking. Afraid to interrupt, I crouched in the hallway and watched them through the open door.

It was a large mirrored room filled with Empire Bombay style furniture. My mother's makeup table was blanketed with jewelry, perfume bottles, make-up and folded lace handkerchiefs. I soon learned the significance of the folded handkerchiefs. She carried one with her at all times. Since Rafael was not only a friend of my father's but did business with him as well, he was a frequent guest in both our home and my father's store. If my mother dropped her lace handkerchief, it was a signal to Rafael that she had time for him and they would meet at the movie theater. It was, for me, a painful occurrence that lasted over many years.

Seated in front of the giant mirror attached to her dresser, she seductively combed her long blonde hair, fully aware that my father spread out in bed watched her through the mirror. Next to his side of the bed, a small table was piled high with books. I waited patiently for them to finish talking so I could approach— too late! The canon went off!

Every night at nine o'clock sharp, a canon is fired. By tradition, el Cañón de las Nueve, a ritual which I'm told continues to this day, started in the late seventeenth century when Spanish colonial officials closed the gates to Old Havana to protect its citizens from pirates and marauders. My parents followed the routine of going to bed immediately upon hearing the canon fire and continued that ritual of nine o'clock bed time until they died.

My father immediately set his watch, crossed his fists over his chest and shut his eyes. My mother slithered into bed and touched my father.

"Tomorrow is a workday," he grumbled.

Clearly disappointed, she mumbled.

"Every day is a workday. I miss you."

"Don't bother me," my father scoffed, "I have business on my mind. You'll have to wait."

Frustrated, she shrieked, "Wait? Wait for what? I waited to marry you. I waited for a child."

My father placed her face in his hands and gently cooed, "How could I marry you without a proper place to live, without money to put food on the table? You question my love?"

"No", she said with a disappointed voice. "Your love-making."

Insulted, he huffed, "I make love to you every day I put a roof over your head and clothes on your back."

My mother was reaching for more. "Do you have to continue to support your sisters and brothers?" she asked him patiently.

"I pay your sister's rent too," he replied, "and feed your brothers. Do you want me to stop taking care of your family as well?" he continued.

"No, they need help and it makes me feel important," she answered.

Softening, he kissed her on the cheek, patted her on the head, and smiling said, "Just make sure you look beautiful for me, keep a clean house, have my meals ready on time and I'll take care of you for the rest of your life."

My mother responded demurely, "Now that Julian will be going to school, I want another child."

He bolted upright. Exasperated, he answered, "You are the most beautiful woman in the world to me, and my love for you knows no boundaries, isn't that enough for you?"

"No, everybody is talking about you, saying that a prosperous man like you should have a big family."

He sneered. "Don't be so sure they are talking about me, you're lucky you got away with this one!"

"Lucky," she answered, "another abortion would have killed me."

While I didn't quite understand what they were talking about, I was uneasy when my father responded in disgust, mocking my mother. "I need money for milk for the baby, clothes for the baby, shoes for the baby."

My mother was disappointed, "I want a big family!"

He was adamant. "No! Another child would tie me up in the pocket! No more pocket dwellers!"

I knew he was talking about me. I scurried to my room, knowing I wasn't wanted, needing my mother's love, desperate for my father's love and thoroughly confused by both of them. I buried my face in my pillow and cried myself to sleep while the arguing continued.

. . .

The next week, like clockwork, my mother had her hair done. While Angelo and I completed a puzzle on the floor, Mara said, "Anita, have you decided on a school for Julian yet?"

"What do you suggest?" my mother purred.

Mara simply replied, "Send him to the school Angelo attends. It's on the way to the movie houses you like to go to."

I began to cry as my mother responded, "What a good idea."

Angelo hugged me and said, "Don't be scared, I'll look out for you at school."

With me off to school, Anita was going to be alone. Arturo was adamant about not having any more children. That conversation was over. Within a week we had a puppy, a cat, a parrot and a goldfish. Anita was building her family inside the home. She treated the puppy like an infant and carried it around like a prop.

"Isn't she cute, Arturo, wouldn't you like a little girl?"

My father huffed his annoyance. The cat knocked an expensive Chinese platter off a shelf; it shattered into a hundred pieces and made a sickening sound. Arturo gave Anita *the silent stare* and by the next morning the cat mysteriously disappeared.

Shortly thereafter he was replaced by a bulldog which became my pal. The parrot took a liking to me as well, and me to him. Anita added parakeets, canaries and a large fish tank. The fish were a constant source of curiosity and enjoyment. My father was happy, my mother ceased her begging for a child, and little money was put out for the pets; the dogs ate scraps, kept the mice, rats and water bugs away, and Woolworth's bird seed and fish food were a cheap enough investment and, according to Arturo, kept my mother occupied. She stayed busy in the house except on the occasional Saturday afternoon when she took me to a movie.

I developed a troubling cough and had difficulty breathing. Arturo reluctantly paid a dollar fifty for me to visit the clinic and I was diagnosed with asthma. He chided me for being weak, complained about the cost of the medicine and shots I had to endure, and blamed me for his misery. I guess the dogs, cat, fish, canaries, parrot, parakeets, mice, rats, water bugs and dust had nothing to do with my condition. I found out years later that I have an allergy to dogs and cats.

One Sunday morning we were all well-groomed and dressed in our best, ready for what I thought was a day out together as a family. Before we left our seven room Mediterranean-style home filled with Louis XIV furniture, overrun with antiques and Catholic religious objects and illuminated by Strauss crystal chandeliers in every room, my parents followed a well-worn ritual of their own. My father in a brown suit and hat methodically unplugged table lamps, wall lamps and chandeliers as he walked through each room. My mother coiffed, overly made-up, and dressed in a tight skirt, low-cut blouse and spiked heels followed behind and closed and locked every window in each room.

I ran around, made believe I could fly, and swooped behind them shouting, "Moon rocket lands on French Empire table next to Murano Lamp touching Baccarat Vase."

Those antiques were also my toys and I am proud to say I have never broken a piece. I have always understood their value and appreciated their workmanship and beauty. My mother screamed at me, "Julian, don't touch the glass!"

"It's not glass, Mama, it's crystal."

She slapped my little hands. "Stop following us. Stand by the door and wait!"

With bowed head, hands behind my back, I obeyed. Anita attempted to get Arturo's attention. "I must have spent two hours curling my hair for you. Do you like it?"

Indifferent, he ordered, "Don't interrupt me. Get the pillowcase."

The pillowcase contained a Wonder Bread wrapper. She removed the Wonder Bread wrapper and waited while Arturo unplugged the telephone and handed it to her. She carefully wrapped the telephone in the pillow case and stored it in the

Wonder Bread wrapper which my father closely inspected. They proceeded to the kitchen where Arturo placed the telephone in the refrigerator.

"Good. They break in, they can't up my telephone bill."

He continued to unplug small appliances and straighten the gas jets. He checked his gold Rolex watch, "I want dinner on the table by six on the dot."

I grabbed onto my father's leg, and begged, "Why can't I go with you, Papa?"

He answered sternly, "Julian, I told you before, no children allowed in the antique market. You belong with your mama."

"I'll be good," I assured him.

He ignored my plea. Of my mother he inquired, "Where are you going today?"

Off handedly, she quipped, "I'll figure out something to keep the boy busy."

An hour later, there I was all alone, kicking pebbles in the park while my mother and Rafael seated on a park bench openly groped each other.

CHAPTER TWO

———————✻———————

July, 1950
Havana, Cuba

The following week, my mother dressed me for our outing; the first stop was my father's store. Cluttered with valuable antiques, furniture, lamps and chandeliers, I was mesmerized by the colors, shapes and textures of each piece. Every square inch of the store was filled with a potential profit maker except one; the third shelf on the back wall—which remained empty. My father instituted a strict rule that not even a piece of paper was to be placed upon it, or else. His workers obeyed. I watched as a young worker swept the floor, arranged and dusted the antiques, and was careful to avoid the dreaded third shelf.

My mother was unusually hurried, so she prompted me to move more quickly as we headed to my father's office in the back of the store. She rang the buzzer outside the gated door. Arturo unlocked the door to the eight by eight windowless room which contained a large desk, a wobbly chair and a huge safe. He ushered us in and quickly locked the door. On the desk was an Astra 6.35 MM caliber 25 Auto Modelo 200 colt pistol next to piles of American five, ten and twenty dollar bills. The safe was wide open, filled to capacity with more cash and jewelry. My father embraced my mother, ignored me and inquired of her, "What now, love of my life?"

"I need another five dollars," she purred.

Arturo filled his fists with money, held it to his nose, inhaled deeply and said, "Ah, money—the smell of it!"

Anita ignored him and continued, "We're going to the movies."

I was not happy. Arturo held onto his money and asked, "Five dollars every week?"

"Well," she replied, "I have to keep your son busy. Must you count every penny?"

"Why not?" he retorted, "it's my money, my store, my house and you know you are just not very good with money."

"Yes, I forgot," Anita answered," money is your true love and I am just your receptacle on occasion.

Arturo removed a five dollar bill from his piles of cash and presented it to her with a flourish and then he looked at her face. "Those frown lines will mar your gorgeous face. Go to your movies."

Arturo studied me for a brief second.

"You, you can count?"

I was ready to show off and started to count on my fingers. He pointed to me and roared, "Make sure she brings home some change."

I took that order to heart and from that day on, I became the designated change overlord. I reminded my mother at every purchase that she had to bring home change. As I aged and was more proficient in handling money, I took care of the transactions and lived in fear of a time when we would not bring home any change.

Arturo fondly kissed her on the lips. He turned his attention back to his money and cooed. It made him happy. Then he pushed us out of the door and locked it. As my mother and I exited the store Rafael, in uniform, ambled in carrying a large box. Anita dropped a lace handkerchief. Rafael picked it up and handed it back to her with a wink and a nod, as he tipped his cap.

"Good day Mrs. Vida."

I bowed my head and avoided him. Outside, my mother dragged me away from the store. We were several blocks away when I boldly declared, "I don't want to go to the movies!" Smack! Then she leaned down and tried to patiently explain.

"Your papa is so important and helps so many people that we have to stay out of his way so he can work and make lots of money to take care of us. And because he is so busy, we have to find something to do and the movies are fun. Do you understand?"

I thought about what she said and was proud of my father, but frightened of Rafael.

"Then why does Rafael have to come with us?" I asked.

"Rafael protects us when your papa can't be with us."

"No!" I yelled and before she could raise her heavy hand. I broke loose, dashed into snarled traffic and scurried back to my father's store. Anita tried to follow me but her tight skirt, high heels and bumper to bumper traffic prevented her from catching me.

I reached the store out of breath and banged as hard as I could on the door to my father's private office. He opened it, gun in hand, and shoved me into a corner while ordering me to keep quiet. Rafael sat behind the desk and leaned back on the wobbly chair with his hands behind his head while my father examined a chandelier perched on the desk. My father inquired, "Brass and glass? You promised me bronze and crystal."

Rafael continued to lean back, rocking to and fro.

"Sorry, that's all I could get my hands on."

Arturo answered confidently, "No deal, return my money."

"It's gone," Rafael calmly said.

Arturo gave him *the silent stare* and suggested, "What if I told your captain you steal from crime scenes?"

Rafael laughed and proclaimed, "Then I would have to report you for buying stolen goods on the black market. Besides, who do you think took the bronze and crystal chandelier?"

Rafael rose out of the chair and my father pushed him back down.

"I want my money now and you're not leaving until I get it."

He aimed his gun at Rafael.

Rafael laughed, "What are you going to do, shoot a cop with that old firecat?"

"Do you want a running start?" my father asked.

Rafael reached for his weapon and shouted, "I am a trained killer!"

I panicked, grabbed my father's leg and cried, "Please don't kill my papa!"

My father shook me off and roared, "Stay in the corner and keep quiet!"

I obeyed. Then with a smooth swift move, my father flipped the wobbly chair, overpowered Rafael and relieved him of his weapon. Rafael scrambled to stand upright. My father had both guns. Rafael, clearly defeated, quietly asked, "Do you think you can really kill a man?"

"Only an evil man," my father answered, "just like my father taught me."

Arturo then told a harrowing story to Rafael, it went like this:

> *"In 1926," he began, "when I turned thirteen, I traveled to a small town outside Havana with Pablo, my father. The old steam train with torn straw woven seats and cracked, dusty windows moved slowly. 'This is not the*

way to the prostitutes,' I said, but Pablo answered, 'Arturo, how would you know?' I kicked the trash away from my feet and replied, 'I'm not the first boy in my class to turn thirteen and you're not the first father to help his son celebrate his manhood.' Laughing, he said, 'Help you? Tonight Arturo, you will help me! And by tomorrow, you will be a man.'

"By the time we reached our destination it was dark. My father pushed me off the train and on to the platform then jumped right behind me. We moved swiftly and silently through sugar cane fields until we came to a small house. My father shoved me to the front door and signaled me to knock while he hid in the shadows. A half dressed man, forty-three, paunchy and slow on his feet, holding a machete opened the door and that's when Pablo forced me aside and kicked the door in.

"My father hurled the man onto a couch, the machete landed on the floor out of reach. My father took a shooting stance. The man held up his hands; he shot him once in each hand. 'That's for the hands that stole my money!' The man screamed, then I screamed, 'Papa, don't kill him!' and I grabbed for the gun. My dad punched me in my stomach so hard that I thought I would vomit. He then turned back to the man on the couch. 'This is for the eyes that stare at my woman.' He shot twice. The man's head snapped back and dropped as he rolled in pain. 'He's dying,' I screamed. I lunged for the gun again and my dad tripped me, sending me crashing into a table. And then he said, 'Just in case,' and emptied the last two bullets into the man's groin.

The man oozed off the couch into a ball of blood and broken body parts.

"There was silence. Pablo quietly exited. I stumbled out of the house after him and found myself on the train. 'Why?' I begged. Calmly and patiently Pablo explained, 'Arturo, it's a man's duty and responsibility to take justice into his own hands to right a wrong. As my business partner, that piece of garbage emptied our entire bank account and stole all of my money, left me, your mother, your sisters and brothers, without a penny. Then he tried to steal your mother. He deserved to die.'

"I asked, 'What if you get caught?' 'Only you and I know what happened, Arturo, and dead bodies don't talk.' We traveled home in silence. Then Pablo said with tears in his eyes 'You will have to leave school.' 'Why, I asked?' 'He stole all our money; I haven't enough left to support us the way we were living.

'So, I've arranged a job for you with an elderly couple who own an antique store. You'll sweep floors and help out. In exchange they will give you a place to live and educate you. I can no longer take care of you. I am proud of you for meeting your manhood tonight.' Pablo gave me his gun. 'I don't want it,' I said. He insisted I take it. 'It will protect you from evil men.' We hugged. It was the only time my father ever hugged me.'"

The story was over. I was too young to grab the significance of all of it at that time, but it is embedded in my memory and over the years has served to give me a better understanding of my own father. Arturo addressed Rafael and said, "And now you know how I learned to take care of people who try to steal from me."

Disheveled and embarrassed, Rafael collapsed in defeat. Arturo waited for him to make a move while I hugged the wall. Arturo stared at Rafael and said quietly, "My money?"

"Enough!" Rafael said.

He took out seventy-five dollars and threw it on the desk. All was quiet. The silence was broken by my mother's frantic knocking on the door. Arturo ignored her. I knew another beating was coming as Arturo picked up the money and fanned his face with it.

"Now remove this shit from my office and start bringing me the good stuff!"

Rafael hurriedly repacked the chandelier into the box. The buzzer was buzzing. Anita's pleas and frenetic knocking continued.

"My gun," Rafael quietly said.

Before returning Rafael's gun to him, Arturo admired his own gun, "Ah, my gun makes me a man, but money makes me a king."

"Guard your castle well, my friend," Rafael then said.

Arturo just laughed, "You are evil, Rafael, and remember what my father taught me—dead bodies don't talk."

I learned more about my father and his relationship with my grandfather than I realized, even though I never met my grandfather, he died before I was born. Sadly, I never met any of my grandparents.

The knocking continued. Arturo opened the door for Anita, frazzled and hysterical. She glared at me and stabbed me with her eyes!

"What did the boy say?" she gasped, wondering what was between Arturo and Rafael.

"The boy?" my dad responded.

He had forgotten I was there still crouched in the corner. Anita peeled me off the wall and quickly realized she was safe. I hadn't said anything. Arturo then opened the door and pushed us all towards it.

"All of you get out! I have no time for your nonsense!"

My mother prodded me towards the exit. Rafael ambled next to us and whispered, "You'll have to pay for the movie for me today. He took all my money."

. . .

September, 1955
Havana, Cuba

At Mara the hairdresser's suggestion, I attended the same school as Angelo. It was a prestigious all boys' parochial school run by priests. I attended from age five to eleven. Angelo was three years ahead of me and I saw him occasionally, which was comforting, however the age difference prevented us from being close friends. I was about ten when one day in the schoolyard, Angelo placed his arms around me and said he would always protect me. However, I realized that Angelo seemed to weaken more and more until finally he was hospitalized for a long period of time. I couldn't get any information from either my mother or father, but among the whispers of neighbors and schoolmates I heard the word cancer.

When Angelo returned to school, he was missing part of his leg. I offered to carry his books, hold his arm, and share my food. He was grateful and kind, but independent and protective. He talked about ultimate freedom and when I asked him what that meant he told me, "Relief from the pain—death."

I asked him what happened to people when they die. He said they don't die. Their spirit lives and travels all over the world searching for people to love and help. I asked him if he would help me and he said, "Of course, just look up and I'll brush you with my wings."

He was at peace, confident in his limited future. That was the last time I saw Angelo. I begged my mother to take me to the funeral, but she refused. Neither she nor my father attended. I was sad, embarrassed and angry.

I moped around the house after Angelo died. Anita actually encouraged me to seek out friends and invite them to the house. One afternoon after school, I invited three schoolmates back to my house. We went to my room and I showed my new friends my coin collection. Then as boys do, we ran down the hall for milk and cookies, then returned back to my room and played with my toys for a while. Arturo was not happy. Apparently four boys running in the hallway shook the ceiling of his store and rattled a few chandeliers and antiques. But the most disturbing part was that some of my coins were stolen.

That night, Anita and Arturo together sat me down—a first! Arturo began, "I understand some coins were taken from you today?"

"I am so sorry Papa," I cried.

He asked me if I knew who took them and I told him I wasn't sure.

Anita then shouted, "No more friends in my house!"

Arturo agreed, "She's not wrong, trust no one; no one is your friend and everyone gets robbed—once, do you understand?"

"I think so," I answered.

My father almost smiled and said, "Yes, you understand."

We never discussed it again and I never had another school friend to my home. That night I prayed to Angelo for freedom and wings, and a small voice down deep said you have many, many years to live. Fear nothing. I felt my hair move, fell asleep and had my first flying dream. Thank you, Angelo!

While I prayed for freedom, the Revolutionaries, Fidel Castro and Frank Pais, joined forces and continued their fight for freedom against the ruling dictator, Fulgencio Batista Zaldívar. Here's what they were fighting about: Batista, who was elected president of Cuba from 1940–1944, and who instituted the Cuban constitution in 1940, returned from the United States in 1952 in order to again run for president. However, fearing an election loss, he led a military coup and remained in power from 1952–1959.

He eliminated the constitution, he was corrupt, and he amassed vast sums of money from the wealthy to whom he awarded lucrative commercial contracts, and to the American Mob, for the freedom to run gambling, drugs and prostitution rings in Havana.

Street demonstrations and student riots protested the wide gap between the poor and the rich. These riots were quickly squelched. Batista censored the media and used the Bureau for the Repression of Communist Activities who resorted to violence against the demonstrators.

My father told me that during that time, although nothing changed in my home or his business, many Cubans hoped that Castro and Pais, both charismatic young men, would bring change to the republic and get rid of the corrupt dictatorship of Batista. It was more like background chatter than daily concern, because the American dollar circulated freely on par with the Cuban peso, and there were no restrictions on travel, dealings with foreign currency and banks overseas, and individuals were free to own and keep whatever one chose, and to live and work where one pleased.

During the school year I would return home for lunch every day. Before I was old enough to walk the three blocks myself, Anita took me back and forth. One day, a few months after Angelo died and the coin calamity, my father closed the store and asked me to accompany him to a bodega for lunch. I was elated. We walked side by side to the bodega, which was near where we lived, and where he ordered a beer. He gave me a sip and tussled my hair; we ate olives and talked about school before we returned home. Arturo walked me back to school that day. I think I grew an inch just from a feeling of great pride and joy.

That year on Christmas morning, I found coins on the floor leading to my room. I was so excited I ran to my father to show him. He ignored me and continued reading his paper. I went to my room and hid them in a special box. The following year, the same thing happened, and every year thereafter. It was never discussed. What a thrill for me to wake up every Christmas morning and find the coins and, until his death just prior to his reaching ninety-five years of age, my father continued to give me coins, many of which I carry to this day.

Christmas presents? That was my mother's job. Every year she took me to Woolworth's and had me choose a toy for Christmas. I put great thought and much joy into my choices. Every year I anticipated receiving my special gift. But, I never received what I chose. She either forgot or deemed it unimportant. It was a great disappointment and I came to hate the ritual but always looked forward to the coins.

My mother and Rafael continued their Saturday afternoon trysts from time to time. One Friday night, I watched as my mother prepared for her Saturday date.

"Come here," she cooed.

I fell into her arms and she hugged me tightly. I thought maybe now the hitting would stop.

"Get a good night's sleep, I have a surprise for you tomorrow," she whispered.

"No more cartoons?" I said too eagerly.

"No more cartoons," she replied.

For the first time, I experienced an inner calm tinged with joy. We hugged, kissed and I went off to bed.

Saturday afternoon, there we were, Rafael, my mother and me at the movies. She was correct—no cartoons. *To Catch A Thief* with Cary Grant and Grace Kelly graced the screen. I sat at the edge of my seat enraptured and never looked behind me. I couldn't wait until I got home to my room. I swept my books aside, stood in front of the mirror, tucked in my shirt, combed my hair and said in perfect English, *"Hello darling."* I knew who I wanted to be and with whom I wanted to be.

· · ·

August, 1956
Havana, Cuba

By this time I was eleven and my mother felt it was time for me to be in a co-ed environment so I wouldn't turn into a homosexual. Why did she think this, or why was she worried? Blame it on the parrot. She thought our parrot was a homosexual because when I returned from school, he sang my name and danced around the cage. So every day I took him out of the cage and placed him on my shoulder. He would nudge my ear and rub his head against my hair; he was very gentle with me.

In stark contrast his behavior towards my mother was harsh. He squawked and bit her every time she tried to clean the cage or place food or water in it. She was not used to rejection. Her beauty was her power and she used it unabashedly. Therefore, she concluded, our parrot was gay and in her twisted mind she feared he would influence me. She never realized that she often hit me in front of him which made him nervous. With each blow, he squawked and rattled the cage. She never noticed. So she pulled me out of the only school I had known and enrolled me in a co-ed school, and while I liked being around girls, the move meant I had to repeat a grade which made me quite bored and unhappy.

During this time, in Mexico City, Fidel Castro, Che Guevara and a group of Cuban revolutionaries were arrested and eventually released.

On a sixty foot yacht named *Granma* headed towards Cuba, Castro led a group of about eighty men. In the province of Santiago de Cuba, about three-hundred young men led by Frank Pais and dressed in olive green uniforms sewn by supporters, attacked police and harbor headquarters as well as the customs house. Rumors swirled that young boys close to my age were being recruited for the revolution.

Rafael visited our home after dinner one night. While I did a puzzle at the table, Rafael and my father smoked cigars and drank espresso. I stayed to keep an eye on Rafael and protect my father. My mother retired to her bedroom. Arturo asked, "What are you hearing about the rebels?"

Rafael took a long puff on his cigar. "They're more trouble than you think, but Fidel was always a rebel."

"Fidel? You know him?" my father inquired.

"Met him once, he went to The University of Havana with my cousin," Rafael answered, "Jorge, who practices law. Jorge told me Fidel always carried a 45 automatic with him all the time. But to answer your question, down at the station, we're hearing more about the skirmishes in the mountains."

I didn't pay much attention to the conversation. I was concerned about my new school which I didn't like. The next day, innocently and with no disrespect intended, I challenged a teacher about an answer to a lesson I had learned in my previous school and was immediately labeled a trouble-maker and reported to the principal as being disrespectful. After having been labeled by the teacher and the principal, the incident continued to grow. I was deemed out-of-control by my mother, who decided I needed more discipline and sent me to a military school where I was to be trained as an army officer.

• • •

March, 1957
Havana, Cuba

I was now twelve years old. The school was far from my home so it was a long day of tedious bus travel and tough military training. By the time I returned home, exhausted, I barely had enough strength to eat quickly, do my homework and get to bed; often before the canon went off. Because I followed my parents' strict orders, I made no friends, just acquaintances.

The one bright spot at school was during lunchtime. I often brought pastries from Benjamin and Ruth, a hardworking couple who operated a small booth in the school yard to sell snacks to instructors, students and staff.

They were physically small of stature but muscular and wiry. I'd say they were in their late thirties, yet hardened by some terrible life event which belied their true age. They seemed haunted and in a constant rush. They moved in sync quickly and efficiently, and were very kind to me.

I soon found out they had a pastry shop near my home. They worked long hours baking the pastries, operating the shop and using the lunch hour to sell their goods at the school; then back to the shop. My parents knew them as the Polacos—to them, all Jews were called Polacos. The Chinese were Chinos and Chinas.

Privately, my parents had derogatory names for everybody, but publicly they were polite and socially gracious, and everyone was addressed formally as senor, senora and senorita. I was trained to be respectful as well. My parents never bothered to learn anyone's proper name. Our neighbors and business associates whom we lived near and worked with for many years were known by the following names:

> El Cojo – man who walks with a limp
> Moscon – old gay guy
> Tortillera – lesbian
> Flaca and flaco – the skinny gal or guy

El bugaron – men who like to give it in the ass
Boca Chula – women who have lips that suck or can be sucked
Fletera – cheap street prostitute
Puta – established prostitute
Chismosa – one who gossips
Bemba – a gossip of unfounded rumors
Chivato – a squealer, an informer
Jamonero – a man who gropes women

After school, I would stop by the bakery before going home, more often to see Benjamin's and Ruth's daughter Irene, than to buy pastries. She was my age, a delicate, slender, blond beauty on the verge of womanhood.

Benjamin's and Ruth's quaint shop, filled with the aroma of freshly baked goods, was warm and inviting. Classical music played on the radio; there were bookshelves to the side filled with maps, history books, literature and the latest magazines; it was such a comfortable environment that it made you feel like relaxing in a chair, with your feet up, reading a book. Benjamin, Ruth and Irene were becoming my friends. I could talk to them about anything, ask them about anything. They were interested in my studies, they were interested in me, and encouraged me to research and learn about anything and everything that intrigued me. They spoke several languages and kept up on world events; they loaned me some wonderful magazines and books.

One day after school, I stopped by on my way home. Ruth was reading an article in *Time Magazine*. She was incredulous and said, "Can you believe this. This journalist traveled to the Sierra Maestra to interview Castro and the rebels?"

Benjamin put his magazine down. "This isn't good," he said, "the future is in doubt—again."

"Is there no peace for us?" Ruth continued, and then turned to me. "Julian, is your father concerned about the guerillas in the mountains?"

I answered simply, "I don't know."

"Didn't you hear about the young boys tortured and killed?" Ruth asked.

I left the store and vowed to learn more about current events. It was only through my model planes and ships, stamp collections, and Benjamin and Ruth's magazines that I traveled the world from my small room. Oh, how I wished I could leave and see the world beyond my parents' building.

My father read *Diario De La Marina* a daily newspaper and two weekly magazines, *Bohemia* and *Cartales*. I made it a habit to do the same, hoping to spark conversation between us. Batista imposed a blackout on the news of battles in Orient Province, but through short-wave radios and gossip it was common knowledge that there were frequent battles between Batista's armed forces and the rebels, and that several members of Batista's government owned Swiss bank accounts rumored to contain millions of dollars. I asked my father if he was concerned and he told me that he trusted no-one, but of the two he trusted Castro less because he hates the rich and that is never good for business.

My father was less anxious when a new Shell Oil refinery was inaugurated by President Batista. The Havana Hilton and Hotel Riviera opened. Celebrities flocked to the island and there were daily reports of lavish parties. It looked like fun. Tourism boomed and my father's business profited. It was well-known that the American Mob operated freely under President Batista's dictatorship. If you didn't bother them, they didn't bother you.

CHAPTER THREE

January 1958
Havana, Cuba

Nineteen fifty-eight was an exciting year for me; mixed with anticipation and fear. I was about to turn thirteen and remembered my father's story about his coming of age at thirteen, and wondered if he would ask me to help him right a wrong like his father had asked him. Instead, he continued to ignore me. Arturo sat in his favorite chair and read *Diario De La Marina*, engrossed in articles about the current political climate. He patted the dogs while he seemed concerned. Anita peered over his shoulder and kept asking, "What does it say?"

He answered, "I'll explain later."

My mother insisted on a birthday celebration and convinced my father it would be good for business.

My parents invited my family, neighbors and business associates over to celebrate my coming of age. Before the birthday, my mother and I made sure the chandeliers shone and the antiques glistened. I had a plan which I worked on for days. There I was, I stopped by the bakery, balancing my books and pretending to search the counters for a pastry. Irene stood erect behind the counter, blushing, patting her pink cheeks and twirling her silken hair.

"Your parents make the best pastries in the world. It is so hard to choose."

Irene smiled with that lovely smile that made her eyes twinkle. Benjamin and Ruth stood aside and kept a close eye on the dance of the innocents.

Benjamin placed his arm around Irene and said, "Thank you, Julian, the usual?"

I stood at attention and practically saluted, "Yes sir!"

Irene placed three pastries in a bag and I paid. Ruth smiled, "How about a chocolate cream cake for your party?"

"Okay, thank you," I agreed.

Then Irene quipped, "When our boys turn thirteen, they become men."

"Then what do your girls become?" I answered perhaps too quickly.

"Young ladies," Ruth answered for her, to which I responded, "Well, young lady, why don't you come to my birthday party Sunday afternoon?"

Benjamin interjected, "Perhaps you should get your parents' permission."

Boldly, I replied, "I don't need their permission, I'm a man now."

I went home and approached Anita in the kitchen and told her I knew what I wanted for my birthday. Distracted, she said half-heartedly, "Tell me."

"Music lessons," I announced.

Anita laughed, made the universal sign for insanity by curling her finger against the side of her head and declared, "Don't be ridiculous! Music will make you insane. You'll go crazy!"

I lost my temper, "Why do you ask me every year what I want and never give me what I want? Why don't you listen to me?"

Unmoved, she answered, "What do you have to say that is so important?"

"Isn't anything I want or think important to you?" I responded.

Off handedly, she quipped, "Of course not, children are to be seen, not heard. I'll tell you what's important!"

I meekly told her that the Polacos listen to me, and that stung. She stopped what she was doing. "You talk to the Polacos? I'm telling your father."

I summoned my courage and told her, "They are my friends."

She was horrified, "You don't need any friends!"

"But I do!" I raised my voice. "Papa won't talk to me; you won't let me out of your sight! You keep me locked up like a virgin girl."

Piqued, she said, "Don't you talk to me in that tone!"

She raised her hand to hit me but I blocked the blow with my forearm. She recoiled in pain.

"Hurt your hand, Mama? Good!"

Defeated, she whispered, "You're strong now, like a man."

That was the last time she tried to hit me.

My elaborate party was a happy event sprinkled with confusion and worry. Happy because I was seeing relatives and a special friend and receiving gifts; confusing for my mother because she was unable to read and was losing her power over me and worried—well all the adults were worried because a charismatic young man named Fidel Castro, his brother Raul and friend Che Guevara, an avowed Communist, continued to lead a revolution that was gaining strength, support and international attention. Those who attended the party were there to help me celebrate my special birthday as well as to pay homage to my father.

The dining room table was set with fine china. A large platter of ham and finger sandwiches graced the table on one side and another with pastries and coffee on the other. My father served champagne. After a while, he led the men into the living room, distributed expensive cigars and led a discussion about the current political climate and how it would affect them personally. I listened intently in between trips to the window; I was expecting Irene. There was a lot of chatter amongst the men, about the Castro brothers causing havoc in the mountains, and the possibility of them marching through the cities. The women wandered in from time to time and seemed anxious. My mother was confused; I kept checking the front door.

I was happy to see my Uncle Pepe, my father's look-a-like younger brother and his wife, Aunt Carmen who was short, round and childless. They were hard-working, simple people clearly in love with each other. They treated everyone with appropriate social graces. Like my parents, in the privacy of their home, they gossiped about everybody and were harshly critical. Pepe picked up the paper and read while my father declared that Castro was like a double edged razor in a dark room.

"I don't trust him. He's not good for business," My father said.

"And that Che Guevara—he's a communist, "Pepe responded, "and they're going hand in hand. What can we expect? Arturo, come with me to Miami, I am going to open an account in an American bank before Carmen and I move to New York."

I piped up, "New York! You mean Manhattan where the Empire State building is?"

"Yes," Aunt Carmen said, "and the Statue of Liberty and the United Nations Building. Come with us," looking at my father she continued, "it's getting too dangerous here."

"Leave my home, my business, never!" Arturo responded.

"At least put your money in American banks," Pepe said.

"My money stays where I can smell it," Arturo patiently replied.

Excitedly, I told my Uncle Pepe that I wanted to go with him, "My English is really good."

I thought I saw a twinge of sadness in my father's eyes and he said to me, "Cuba is your home. You belong with your mother. Besides, they won't be gone long."

"How do you know?" Carmen said.

"You are just a watchmaker," Arturo said to Pepe, "you can't even afford these pastries."

It was cruel and embarrassing.

I paced by the door, peered out the window and relaxed. I watched as Irene, Ruth and Benjamin approached the house. Just then a single engine plane buzzed overhead and dropped leaflets which blanketed the street. My relatives ran to look through the windows. While Ruth picked up a leaflet I saw Benjamin hand Irene the cake, kiss her on the cheek, and turn to leave. The bell rang.

"I'll get it," I shouted and scurried down the stairs to help Irene and to pick up leaflets for everybody.

Irene and I waved and watched Benjamin and Ruth head home arm in arm hunched over the leaflet. Suddenly they stopped and seemed to react with fear. I quickly picked up as many leaflets as I could and mumbled, "My relatives want to know what's going on."

Irene stood aside and said, "Of course."

We both blushed. Hi was all we could say to each other. It was the first time we were alone and stood so close without a display case and parents standing between us. For a long moment we stared at each other and remained oblivious to the plane, the leaflets, and the funny faces pressed against the windows of our townhouse. I took the cake from her and gently guided her upstairs.

My mother was at the door as Irene and I entered our home. I ushered her in.

"Come in Irene," I said.

"Thank you, Julian, for inviting me. Hello, Mrs. Vida. You have a lovely home; my parents send their regards. Hello everybody, I'm Irene, Julian's friend."

I smiled and handed the cake to my mother. She was stunned, unable to speak, she glared at Irene. Then I took Irene's hand, it felt like a soft glove. She smelled so good. My relatives gathered around and mumbled greetings. I handed out the leaflets I picked up from the street.

Pepe read aloud from the leaflet, *"Down with Batista! Long live the Revolution!"* In the midst of the chatter, Aunt Carmen approached us and graciously introduced herself.

"Hello dear, I am Julian's Aunt Carmen and this is my husband, Julian's Uncle Pepe. It is so nice to meet you."

Irene curtsied, "Likewise," she responded. Then she turned towards me. "My parents made you a special cake," she said, and kissed me on the cheek. I was in heaven. My mother gasped and almost dropped the cake! Aunt Carmen led my mother to the dining room table and all the women fussed over the pastries and prepared the cake as they whispered and giggled.

Arturo and the other men were reading the leaflets, chomping on their cigars, and arguing fiercely when my father spotted the cake. He went to the dining room table and announced, "These are the most expensive pastries in Havana!"

"We know," Uncle Pepe said. My father suddenly realized Irene was attached to my hand.

"What is the little Jewess doing here?" he said.

I stood tall and spoke up, "She is my friend and I invited her." He gave me *the silent stare.* I stood my ground. Hushed silence, *no one spoke up to Arturo.*

Irene added, "My parents send their best regards and thank you for your continued business, Mr. Vida. You are a most valued customer." She curtsied. Arturo smiled. Business he understood. Irene was smart and fearless and I was proud.

My Aunt Carmen said, "Why don't we open the gifts?"

"Not now," I replied and turned on the radio. In front of everyone, I bowed and asked Irene to dance; she curtsied and we floated to the music.

"What a good idea," my Aunt Carmen said and she and Uncle Pepe danced. Other's joined in. Arturo and Anita stood silent; the collective glare was blinding. I twirled Irene, dipped her and held the pose. Aunt Carmen clapped with glee.

My mother said, "Where did you learn how to dance?"

I gave her a knowing glance and said with some sarcasm, "American movies!"

That night, I lingered in the doorway of my parents' bedroom and watched as my mother folded her handkerchiefs. My father paced. I entered and said, "Thank you for my party. I had fun."

My mother sneered, "So, you have a new woman in your life?"

I kissed my mother on the cheek and replied, "She's just a friend, Mama."

My father interjected, "You can't trust them."

To which I responded, "I like them."

He was adamant. "They are setting you up, they're after my money!"

My mother added, "Get rid of her. You don't need girlfriends."

I was defiant. "The only friends I have are my books. You don't let me go anywhere. What am I, your prisoner?"
My father said, "You have your mother. That's enough for you."

He exited the room and I added under my breath, "You're enough for everybody!"

She raised her hand to strike. I said, "Are you sure you want to do that?" She lowered her hand, "Get out!" she said quietly.

• • •

March, 1958
Havana, Cuba

All businesses continued to operate. My father was able to buy and sell real estate, operate his antique business, import chandelier parts from Austria and Czechoslovakia, and export lamps and antiques to South America and the United States. He acquired all required licenses and permits, paid his taxes and ran his business as he saw fit, with no government interference. But the climate was changing. Forty-five civic organizations including lawyers, doctors, architects, engineers, social workers, professors and other professionals signed an open-letter supporting the rebels.

No more music, no more open doorways or friendly conversation. Gossip stopped and fear ruled the streets. Our neighbors were disappearing and those who remained were acting suspicious, whispering, holding secret meetings, and down-sizing, anticipating great change. Everyone seemed as upset as Irene's mother and father were the day they saw the flyer.

I did not understand, nor was any of it of importance to me at age thirteen. I stayed away from the bakery to appease my parents. I saw Benjamin and Ruth at school at lunchtime but our conversations, while cordial, were brief. Then one day, they were gone from the schoolyard. I intended to visit the bakery but I didn't need the distraction or grief from my parents. My courses were becoming more difficult, the military training more intense.

One day, Uncle Pepe came by to share photos of their vacation to Miami. I was mesmerized.

My uncle was at the table with me, just the two of us, and he said out of concern, "Julian, don't you ever leave the house?"

"Not unless I go to school or shop with Mama," I replied. He rubbed my head and went into the other room to speak to my father.

When he returned he said, "Julian come to my house tomorrow night. I want to show you my camera and how to take photos." I went there for dinner and my uncle introduced me to cameras and photography. A few days later Uncle Pepe took me to a camera store and helped me choose my first camera, a Contax IIA. It was an expensive camera for a kid to have.

When it was time to pay, my uncle said to the owner, "Don't worry, his father could buy the block. Just send the bill to Arturo Vida."

The owner bowed and said, "Of course, my pleasure." I had a new hobby, fine equipment and remain forever grateful to my uncle.

. . .

A few days later a national strike which failed due to the lack of popular support caused a serious setback for the rebels. Battista launched a vast offensive against the guerillas in the mountains, the rebels retaliated, the fighting became more violent, and the reporting became more frequent. Military drills at school were longer and more challenging. At the end of every school day, every class of students of every age gathered in the courtyard to march and practice drills with wooden rifles before we boarded our buses to return home.

We were all assigned a number and that is how we were addressed; mine was #3213. One day after a drill, my number was called aloud and it was announced to the entire student body that I was assigned guard duty, school-speak for disciplinary action. I had been accused of a crime against another student and was about to be punished in public for a crime I did not commit.

I was prevented from boarding the bus home. I had no idea what the crime was. I was innocent, but forced to stand at attention for over an hour while the school contacted my parents to pick me up. My father arrived, claimed me from the commander and I was released to his custody fatigued, hungry and over-heated. We went home in silence.

At home, he sat me down and demanded, "Tell me what happened today."

I shrugged my shoulders and said simply, "I was accused of a crime I did not commit." I was too tired to say anymore or to eat so I was sent to bed. I went to school the next day and endured the humiliation of the previous day's events and the uncomfortable stares of my classmates, who shunned me *en masse*. I still had no idea what happened.

Unbeknownst to me, my father went to the commander's office and demanded to know what I was accused of and by whom. The commander called the accuser to the office and he was shown my photo. He confirmed my story and said it was Cadet #3231, not #3213. The clerk who took the report had reversed the numbers. A new report was issued, my name cleared, my father was satisfied; I was growing angry but had no outlet for my feelings. School was hard and I was still paying for someone else's bad behavior, and I stopped my budding relationship with Irene. I still had no life outside of home. I focused on my books and stamps, my only friends. About a week later, Arturo and Anita sat me down for a talk. "Now what," I thought.

Arturo began, "Son, I notice you are losing weight, are you happy at school?"

"I don't think about it," I replied. Anita was silent. Clearly they had something on their minds.

Arturo continued, "I don't think the political climate is conducive to you being in a military school right now."

"What did he know," I thought.

Then Anita chimed in, "Where would you like to go to school?"

I knew exactly. "I want to attend the Bi-lingual Business Academy around the corner where all classes are taught in Spanish and English; I can continue my French studies at the American Institute after my classes; I could help you in the store with the tourists."

Arturo seemed to like that idea.

"Good!" Anita said as if a weight had been lifted, "You will be like your father—a business man."

It was time to see Benjamin, Ruth and especially Irene and tell them what was going on in my life. I hurried to the bakery. It was evening, the store was dark and the shelves were empty. I peered through the glass and knocked on the door. The lights went on.

Benjamin came to the door, "Oh, Julian," he said, "come in. I'll get pastries for your parents."

"No I said, "They can't know I am here. I came to tell you news." Benjamin shut the lights. "Come to the back." I had never been to the back before; it was where they lived. I was shocked and saddened. Suitcases lined the walls, the shelves were empty. Irene and Ruth were packing dishes in large boxes. Irene looked up, startled and dropped a dish. I picked it up for her. She seemed disappointed in me.

"Thank you Julian, but where have you been?"

Lamely, I responded, "Busy, I am sorry." Yes, she was angry.

Ruth and Benjamin respectfully stood aside, gave us our space and as always kept a careful eye on us. Irene challenged me, "Sorry, sorry for what?"

I was having my first tiff with my first girlfriend who gave me my first kiss and my first dance. I was honest, "For not coming by to see you."

She surprised me with her response. "It was the dance, wasn't it?"

I understood her deep hurt. She understood mine so I was able to tell her the truth. "It made my mother nervous."

Ruth hugged me and said, "It doesn't matter anymore, we're leaving."

With a lump in my throat, I asked, "Where are you going?"

Benjamin answered for all of them. "To Israel, we don't trust Castro *or* Batista."

"I'd like to go with you," I blurted out.

Benjamin placed his arms around me and with a heavy heart said, "For many reasons that would not be possible." Irene started to cry.

"Why?" she wept.

Ruth put her arms around both of us while Irene and I held hands.

Ruth kissed us both, wiped our tears and said, "Children—your dreams are so pure. You have very long lives and fascinating roads ahead of you. Perhaps you will meet again."

Gently, Benjamin prodded, "You had better go home now."

Irene and I hugged; our tears moistening each other's' faces. We pulled apart and Irene walked me to the door and before she locked it she said softly, "I'll write to you soon."

We kissed softly on the lips. I ran home, hopped the stairs to my room, cleared my books, looked into the mirror, combed my hair and said, "Goodbye, darling." I cried myself to sleep.

• • •

That weekend Uncle Pepe and Aunt Carmen visited and announced they were moving to America. Arturo was visibly angry.

"So, you abandon your family, I won't have it!"

Pepe responded, "It is not your decision."

Aunt Carmen, always the peace-maker, said joyfully, "Come to the airport to see us off. It would mean so much to us."

"Can we, Papa?" I asked enthusiastically.

Shortly thereafter, there we all were at Rancho Boyeros Airport in Havana standing in silence. There was so much to say but none of us could come up with anything appropriate.

I said innocently, "Will we ever see you again?"

Pepe placed his arm around me and said, "When you get to Manhattan."

Arturo responded, "Then this is good-bye my brother." He and his brother hugged and held onto each other for a long moment. Then we all hugged and wiped our tears. Arturo removed an envelope from his pocket filled with cash.

He gave it to Pepe and said, "Take it, it's a gift."

Carmen said, "Thank you. We can use it."

Arturo replied, "Use it to come home."

We waited until they boarded the plane and waved as it took off to America. I was learning about loss; it was painful.

The battles in the mountains were lasting longer, and according to news reports mixed with gossip, more men were dying every day—some my age. I was upset. The rebels set up Radio Rebelde and broadcast the text of *The Caracas Pact*, which called for an armed insurrection, so Castro and his followers could set up a provisional government and end American support for Batista. Routine in the Vida household was unchanged.

It was Saturday. My mother, father and I were eating breakfast. My mother was ready to go out, "Julian, are you ready?"

I stood my ground, "I'm not going with you today," and before she had a chance to react, I turned to my father and said, "Papa, I would like to spend time with you today."

He peered at me over the newspaper and calmly said, "I open the store at nine, be ready to work." I was thrilled for so many reasons.

I walked into the store promptly at nine and my father greeted me with a broom in hand. "Start in the front," he said. I resolved to do the best I could do and proceeded to sweep. From a short distance behind me, I heard, "You missed a spot."

I put the broom down, "Papa, this is not what I meant when I said I would like to spend time with you. Can't we go out together?"

My father was incredulous, "Where?"

I too was at a loss. "What do other fathers do with their sons? Go to baseball games, the beach. I don't know."

My father turned his back and muttered, "Waste of time." I continued to sweep.

Several pieces of mail were delivered. My father thanked the mailman and focused on each envelope. I stopped to stare at the empty third shelf on the back wall. It gave me time to think. An idea popped in my head and I blurted out, "I can do business with you." I couldn't tell if he was amused or intrigued, but he put the envelopes down and gave me *the silent stare.*

"What business?"

I was confident, "Let me sell my stamps here!"

He rubbed his chin and said quietly, "I'll think about it." I was elated. I swept with great enthusiasm. My father continued to read the mail when I saw him concentrate on what looked like an air mail envelope. He stared at me, fanned his face then ripped it to shreds and threw it in the garbage.

I remembered Irene's promise to write and innocently asked, "Did I get any mail?"

He said quietly, "No." Just then an explosion shook the building. My father and I ran into the street. The sewer had been bombed. There was chaos. Sirens wailed, people were running in all directions, shouting, crying. Arturo checked the outside of the building for damage.

Satisfied that all was well, he said "It's just the rebels and their reign of terror. Help me clean up inside." I obeyed and picked up a couple of broken pieces. I placed them in the trash and saw the air mail envelope torn to shreds. It was from Israel.

I had no chance to react because we heard a second explosion in the distance. Arturo was angry now. He grabbed the broom and cleaned the debris from the outside as I continued to clean the debris from the inside. Seething with anger over the destruction of my letter from Irene, I was composing a rant in my head when after a while one of our neighbors ran by shouting, "The rebels bombed the movie theater!" My father turned pale and stood mute. Did he know? My grave disappointment turned to fear. My heart skipped a beat—my mother!

"I'm going to see what happened." I dashed from the store to the movie theater, fighting the crowds running in the opposite direction away from the theater.

Among the rubble and smoke, I saw Rafael herding people away from the scene. I grabbed him by the collar and screamed in his face. "Where is she?"

He bowed his head, pointed to an alley and said, "She's okay." Relieved, I found her, disheveled and hysterical. I held her close.

She cried, "Don't tell your father." She grabbed my shirt and said, "Promise me, you will never tell your father!" She collapsed in my arms and wept uncontrollably.

"I promise," I reluctantly whispered. I checked her for wounds; she was unhurt, just shaken and frightened. I held her for a long time.

She swooned, "I love him, you know."

I stared directly at her and asked, "Who, Mama, who do you love?" No answer. She seemed faint.

I shook her gently, tapped her face, "I'll take you to a doctor." She half smiled and mumbled, "Help me up. I'm fine." She straightened her clothing, removed a compact from her pocketbook, and fixed her make-up. I watched as she combed her hair.

Once I was sure she was steady on her feet, I murmured, "I'll take you home." I never received an answer to my question nor do I have any idea what she told my father, but when we arrived home, he took her upstairs and gave me the keys to the store so I could finish straightening up and lock up.

· · ·

I enjoyed school and continued my bi-lingual studies. On the weekends I worked in my father's store. He gave me a small space in the front window to display a portion of my stamp collection. About a month after the bombing, I was in the store watching Arturo wire a chandelier. I dusted the antiques and bypassed the long empty shelf on the back wall.

"Why don't you ever use that shelf?" I asked. "I think the new lamps would look nice there."

Without any discernible emotion, he replied, "That's where I slept for the ten years I apprenticed here. It's all mine now. I own it all."

Intrigued, I asked "How old were you?"

He answered simply, "Thirteen."

He didn't seem to mind my questions so I continued, "Why?"

He stopped what he was doing and sat down. "Come here, son." I'm going to tell you a story—once, and then we never talk about it again. I obeyed and sat next to him. He began telling me the story of his father and him; the same story he had told Rafael about his father's partner who robbed him of all his money.

"I know, Papa," I said.

"How do you know? I never told you this story."

"No, not me, you told Rafael."

"The only time I told Rafael was when he tried to sell me crap and called it gold. You were there?" He didn't remember. "Oh well." he continued. "But my father tracked him down and well if you heard the story, you know what happened. But maybe you didn't hear this part. On the way home my father told me he couldn't support me, my mother and my five brothers and sisters. Everything was gone. We had already sold everything we had, moved to smaller quarters and were collecting lemons and limes from the gutter for food. He just couldn't get back on his feet so he made arrangements for me to live with the childless couple who owned this business.

"They lived in a tiny apartment nearby and rented the space for the store. They didn't have any room for me to sleep so they fixed a space here on that shelf," as he pointed to it, "and took me in. I watched over the store for them. After working many years, I saved my money and bought not only the business from the couple when they retired, but I also purchased the building from the landlord."

"Didn't you go to school?" I asked.

"I didn't have to," he replied. They were both school teachers who tutored me daily in all subjects. Literature was my favorite subject, especially poetry." Arturo began to recite:

> *"Youth, divine treasure, already you leave to not return! When I want to cry, I do not cry...and at times I cry without wanting to...."*

He stopped, reached for a book and said, "Here, familiarize yourself with the writings of Ruben Dario—after you finish your work." I was astounded. I went back to sweeping the back of the store. I had a new reverence for the third shelf and made sure it remained spotless.

Just then, an elderly, well-dressed American man came into the store. My father went to work, "Good morning, sir, how may I help you?"

The man pointed to the window and said in decent Spanish, "Show me those stamps in the window."

My father bowed slightly and to my surprise said, "I'll get you the owner." My father came over to me and whispered, "Put down the broom, you have a customer." My first customer; I was proud. I followed my father to the front of the store and mimicked his salesman's behavior. My father stepped aside and said to the gentlemen, "This young man is the owner."

I stepped up, shook the man's hand and said, "Hello sir, how may I help you?"

The man, clearly amused, said, "I understand the stamps are yours."

"Yes, sir and I have more in the back."

The man sat down and said, "Let me see them all." I arranged all my stamps on the table, organized by country, neatly displayed, and well-priced. The man studied them closely and made some notes on a small pad he carried. Arturo stood aside but kept a wary eye on the transaction.

After a long period of time, the man asked, "Are your prices firm?"

I responded with pride, "It depends on how many you buy. I will consider a trade."

He thought about it for a moment, referred to his notes and simply said, "How much of a discount will you give me if I buy them all?" I glanced at my father—he was impressed.

I thought for a moment and said, "Twenty percent."

The man made a note, looked up and said, "That's fair. Will you take a check?"

Without hesitation, I said, "No sir, cash only."

He laughed heartily and in English said, "You drive a hard bargain, boy, it's a deal!" He removed a wad of cash from his pocket and peeled off several bills. I gathered the stamps and carefully placed them in a large envelope. We shook hands.

In English I replied, "Thank you, mister. Please, you are welcome to come back."

"I'll be back," he replied and left the shop.

I fanned out the money and said, "Papa, I doubled my money!"

Stoically he said, "When a man talks to you about payment, don't discuss a trade unless you can't agree on a price." I went back to my sweeping.

. . .

The fighting in the mountains escalated and as Castro's guerillas triumphed in the small towns, they redistributed the land amongst the peasants. In return the peasants either helped the guerillas or joined Castro's army as did students from the cities. The United States' government was not happy with Batista's handling of Castro and his failure to control him or end the conflict. They suggested he hold an election. He did, but the people refused to vote and boycotted the election. This gave Castro the confidence to move forward with a head-to-head battle.

After consultation with members of the United States government, which denied him asylum, as did Mexico, Batista opted to flee Cuba for the Dominican Republic and where he stayed for a short time. His generals attempted to set up another military government and failed. The people were ready for change. Castro called for a general strike and this time he was successful. December 31, 1958, my parents and I gathered around the television set to watch the New Year's festivities. By tradition, my mother set out three dishes, each with twelve green grapes for us to eat as the clock struck midnight and the New Year began.

Las doce uvas de la suerte, meaning the twelve grapes of luck, is a Spanish tradition dating back to the eighteen nineties but officially recognized from 1909 when there was an abundant harvest in Spain and the vine growers popularized the custom in order to sell large amounts of grapes. The tradition started in Spain at the Puerta del Sol Tower Clock in Madrid and spread to Hispanic communities throughout the world. The idea is that as the twelve bells strike at midnight, December thirty-first, a grape is eaten at each strike to represent good luck for each month of the coming year.

Variations I've heard over the years include:

- Standing on your right foot while eating the grapes will help you start the year on the right foot.
- Making a wish as you eat each grape will help your wishes come true in the New Year.
- Finishing the grapes before the New Year will ward off witches and evil spirits.

The tradition continues at the Clock Tower from where the change of year is broadcast, much like the ball drop at Times Square in New York. As we watched the celebration of the defeat of Batista, my father threw out the grapes and went to bed.

CHAPTER FOUR

January, 1959
Havana, Cuba

On the first of January, Che Guevara led the rebels into Havana. A few days later, around my fourteenth birthday, Castro marched into Havana. The streets were filled with jubilant well-wishers, the mood was celebratory. Promising transparency in the new government, Castro vowed to remove all American influence and corruption, along with The Mob, from the island. It was widely reported that United States Companies owned approximately forty percent of the Cuban sugar lands, most of the cattle ranches, about ninety percent of the mines and mineral concessions, eighty percent of the utilities, and most of the oil industry; while the U.S. provided about sixty percent of Cuba's imports. The profits from these interactions increased the wealth and quality of life for the Americans and for Cubans in the cities, but in contrast, about one third of the Cuban population, the residents of the outlying areas, lived in poverty. Most were illiterate. It was here Castro concentrated his efforts and held great influence over the people by defiling the rich.

Castro was going to institute agrarian reform which meant redistributing agricultural land to poor Cubans. He promised equality to all Cubans, for the people, by the people, and proclaimed *"Cuba for the Cubans."* There was no celebration in my house, no gifts; my birthday passed quietly.

Nightly, my mother, father and I gathered around the television and watched Cuba's new leader, Fidel Castro, claim the triumph of the revolution. Both my mother and I tried to engage my father in conversation; we asked questions. My father was silent. He seemed focused on a plan of his own. He made frequent notes, studied them, and then burned them. I continued my studies at the Bi-Lingual Business Academy, but noticed that many of my American teachers were gone and several classmates disappeared as well. If I asked someone what happened to so and so, I was greeted with shrugs and feigned ignorance. People were actually afraid to communicate.

I was sweeping the floors in the store one day and said to my father, "Many of Castro's goals seem good for the people, like the agrarian reform."

He responded thoughtfully, "Yes, it is good for the poor to own land and have a chance to grow and prosper, but are they qualified?"

I asked him, "What do you mean, Papa?"

My father replied, "Do they have the necessary skills to take over a business that may have taken years to develop? For instance, say I hand you the keys to this store that I have invested my entire life and say to you, 'it's yours.' Would you know what to do on a daily basis, on a quarterly basis, on an annual basis to sustain it?

"Do you understand the legalities, the need for licenses to operate, import and export goods? Do you understand bookkeeping and accounting? Can you do payroll? When and how would you pay your taxes? Where and how would you purchase your stock? Who are your suppliers? What is your business plan for the next five years? How and where do you advertise? Do you understand that it took me years to develop the skills and relationships I needed to build this business?" He was turning red. I was dazzled and confused.

I knew I had a lot to learn, "I think I understand Papa."

He went on, "Then what happens to the person who may have saved for years to purchase that land legally, invested many more years of hard work and sacrifice to bring that land to profit? What happens to him and his family when he is displaced and loses everything he worked for? Because a new government said we need to be equal? We'll be equal alright. We'll all be equally poor!" I knew he was talking about himself.

Within a short time, the executions began. Throughout the island, members of Batista's police force, guards, government officials, and military leaders faced firing squads after being prosecuted by military tribunals set up by Castro. Their personal property was confiscated and redistributed. The general population was happy; groups of ten to twenty people ran through the streets screaming, "*Paredon!*" which loosely translates to a thick wall. In that context it meant put them against the wall for the firing squad. Castro declared that the trials would continue until all criminals of the Batista regime were tried. Photos published in the daily press showed not the end, but the beginning of the atrocities committed by the new regime.

Within three weeks Castro held a public military tribunal in a sports stadium in Havana. In front of eighteen thousand spectators and three-hundred reporters, a major from Batista's army was sentenced by three judges to death. Women banded together to protest the executions. By March almost five hundred "war criminals" were executed by firing squads; there were calls for the executions to be stopped. They were suspended during Easter week.

The executions and public trials continued and were reported daily. My father kept the store open beyond his usual closing time to sell his goods. From then on, the only form of payment he accepted was cash. He converted the cash to gold, jewelry, gold coins and pocket watches. He did not replace his stock. He instructed me not to clean the antiques and literally let the dust settle. In the back of the store, we had work benches and parts which were used to fix chandeliers and repair the antiques. The parts and tools were brought to the front of the store so the store looked like a material parts house, not the profitable, prestigious antique store it had been for over twenty-five years.

Castro visited the United States and insisted he was not a communist. A couple of months later, Che Guevara made the first official contact with the Soviet Union. It had become illegal to own foreign currency with a penalty of imprisonment if the money was not turned over to the authorities. Loudspeakers atop trucks often traveled through the streets blasting Castro's speeches similar to the following: *We have confiscated every American property on the island. We have taken back the casinos, the sugar mills, banks and everything foreign owned. American dollars rule here no more. Anyone caught with dollars will go to jail.*

One day, my father received a call from the bank. He was told that by order of the minister of the interior he was to come to the bank and open his safe deposit box in front of officials, and turn over any foreign currency to them. He appeared at the bank as requested; an armed militia man stood by as he opened his safe deposit box and removed a stack of cash. The first bill was an American one dollar bill. The rest of the bills were Cuban currency. The official confiscated the single one dollar bill and replaced it with the equivalent of one Cuban peso. When the official asked my father why he had an American one dollar bill, he replied, "It was a souvenir."

Rafael ran a black market scheme whereby he accepted American money for food and medicine, both of which were becoming scarce. My father used his American money to buy food through Rafael's network of black marketers. He also exchanged American currency and antiques for gold and coins. By the end of the year, the revolution moved to a Marxist-Leninist political system. All United States businesses and properties were nationalized. Castro signed the Agrarian Reform Act and confiscated thousands of acres of farmlands and redistributed them to the poor. He forbade foreign land ownership.

• • •

January, 1960
Havana, Cuba

For my fifteenth birthday, there was no celebration at all. By 1960, the Committee for the Defense of the Revolution (CDR) was established so that everyone's activities were carefully monitored and recorded block by block. CDR officials kept detailed files on every individual residing on their block, which included the daily activities, relationships and details of each household. Neighbor spied on neighbor. Mr. Costas was assigned as our block watcher. It was a good choice. Mr. Costas was about ten years older than I, and lived two houses down from us. His parents lived behind the small grocery store that they owned.

Mr. Costas used to be known as little Mr. Costas. He was a crippled child, wore heavy leg braces and spent many hours sitting in front of his parents' store watching everyone else's life go by, and growing fatter by the year.

He rarely ventured off the block. He knew everyone, spoke to everyone and took a great interest in everyone's lives. He was happy to continue his activity for the revolution. Castro also instituted a law whereby he limited the amount of money a family was allowed to have. If anyone was caught with more than their allotted share, they would be punished. Often that meant prison.

My father called Rafael to the store. The conversation was brief. As Rafael left the store, he turned to my father and said, "It's too dangerous! My advice is to flush it! It's not worth going to jail for worthless Cuban currency."

By order of Mr. Costas, our official for the Committee for the Defense of the Revolution, we now had to record the time we left and returned to the area. I wanted to take pictures of the Morro Castle, so I reported to Mr. Costas when I left, and suggested a time I would return. Dusk was approaching so I walked home and as I approached my house, I saw smoke emanating from our kitchen window. I ran as fast as I could. Just as I was about to reach my house, I was grabbed by the arm and pulled to a stop by our CDR official, Mr. Costas.

"Where are you going boy?" asked Mr. Costas.

"Home, Mr. Costas, I am late for dinner." He held tighter. Please, Mr. Costas, you know how angry my mother gets."

"Tell me where you were and whom you spoke to today or I'll contact the G2 and it is off to jail for you."

"For what?" I asked.

"An invasion is imminent. How do I know you're not part of it?"

"Because you know me and I am not!" I shot back. He referred to his clipboard and made a note. I started to move and he shoved me against the wall.

"Not so fast, I'm not finished."

He looked me up and down. "To me those shoes look American-made." I panicked.

They were. I pulled them off and said, "Here, take them."

Mr. Costas inspected them and said, "Hmm, Florsheim, not bad. You can go now." I sprinted up the stairs in my stocking feet. Breathless, I reached the kitchen; shocked by what I saw. There were two buckets. One filled with water; one filled with fire. My mother threw cash into the fire. My father, weak and pale, just stared at the smoke. They hadn't noticed me until I shouted.

"What are you doing? You can see the smoke from the street!"

My father became alert and said, "Shut up, they will hear you!" He poured water on the fire.

The bell rang and Mr. Costas shouted from the street. What's that smell up there? Is something burning?"

My mother leaned out the window, full cleavage in view and purred, "Nothing to worry about, Mr. Costas. A rag caught fire. Everything is fine now." Mr. Costas was pleased.

Rumors of an American invasion continued to spread. Everyone was on alert. A new directive came down from Castro that anyone with gold was to turn it over to the government for the revolution. There were rumors about armed militia men and women having metal detectors and roaming through homes and businesses unannounced looking for gold, coins, etc., to be confiscated for the revolution. My father hid his gold, jewels and cash behind the kitchen tiles which lined the wall behind a pot rack. One day, two armed militia men came to the store, a grizzled rebel fighter and a young recruit. The older man said to my father, "There are rumors you are hiding gold. Do you mind if we look around?"

My father was very cool, "Not at all. You will find I always obey the rules."

The young recruit asked, "Who's upstairs?"

My father responded, "My wife. She is cooking dinner. I'll tell her you are coming up."

My mother was in the kitchen cooking dinner. She had removed her watch to wash some dishes and placed it on the counter. The militia men searched the house and left, satisfied that nothing was hidden. My mother's watch disappeared. Who could she complain to? Anyone deemed behaving against the revolution was punished, which included simple conversation.

One of our neighbors made the mistake of speaking against Castro in the street and was overheard by the CDR who reported him to the authorities. He was whisked off the street one day and never heard from again—until many decades later—when we found out he had been imprisoned and tortured just for expressing his opinion. All citizens were expected to work one day a week for the revolution. That meant if you were a teacher Monday through Friday, then Saturday you picked sugar cane.

From my father's doorway I watched the rebels comb the streets for anti-revolutionaries. Che Guevara was a frequent visitor to *Informacion*, a local newspaper which operated near my father's business. I watched from the doorway as he arrived on several occasions to the throngs of worshipers. It was an event; he arrived in a jeep surrounded by armed bodyguards. The guards stood aside and allowed the people to flock to him as if he were a rock star. I always kept my distance and remained in my father's doorway. Che noticed me one day because I did not move from my father's doorway or shout "*Long Live the Revolution.*" He motioned me over to him. My neighbors were impressed; Mr. Costas was impressed. I was terrified, but obeyed out of fear, and as I approached, the crowd parted and I extended my hand to shake his.

He was unkempt, un-bathed and utterly charming. He shook my hand, put his arm around me and announced *Venceremos! We shall overcome.* The crowd cheered. I eyed my father watching from across the street. More terrified of my father than Che Guevara, I went home, showered and hid in my room until dinner. With great anticipation I faced my father at the dinner table.

He half smiled at me and said, "You handled that well."

• • •

January, 1961
Havana, Cuba

United States President Dwight D. Eisenhower closed the American Embassy and severed diplomatic relations with Cuba. The middle class Cubans were not happy with Castro's government; many professionals left the island and relocated to Florida. My school was in chaos. Several teachers left as did many students. My parents pulled me out, but no one ever came to look for me. I stayed home and helped my parents. Our country was in transition.

The next day Rafael came to the store, and he and Arturo went to the back office. As many times as I saw Rafael, I never acknowledged him; I always found something else to do. Nor did I ever forgive him. I continued to protect my father, remembering my mother's threat that he would shoot my father dead and it would all be my fault, so I never revealed to my father what I knew. Through the years, Arturo and Rafael continued their business dealings and a quiet friendship. They both distrusted Castro and that seemed to bring them closer.

"I can get your jewels and coins out of the country, "Rafael informed Arturo."

"Can you get them to New York?"

"Through my connections, yes, anywhere in the world."

Arturo said, "Okay, see to it!"

Then Rafael said, "Someone has to make the pick-ups."

"Julian will handle it," Arturo replied.

"You may be putting him in great danger."

"No more danger than being drafted into Castro's Army. Now, what about my cash?"

"We've got banks in Canada and the United States."

"How about Manhattan?"

"Of course, the going rate is twelve to one."

"So if I give you sixty thousand pesos, you'll deposit five thousand U.S. dollars for me?"

Rafael made a note and said, "Correct."

"Make it ten thousand U.S. dollars," Arturo said. That night, just before the canon went off, I heard my father tell my mother, "I'm sending Julian out of the country."

"No," she cried, "he's just a baby."

My father responded, "Do you want your baby in Castro's army?"

Anita whimpered, "Of course not!"

Arturo roared, "Call your cousin in Spain, I have a plan." Arturo never shared his plan with me but there were several letters to Vargas and Gracie, who were Anita's cousins in Madrid, Spain. Arturo took a sudden interest in my school photos and sent one to Vargas. Anita went through my closet and chose slacks and shirts. She started sewing my clothes, opening seams and resewing them. I had no idea what she was doing, nor did I care. I had long ago stopped trying to figure out my mother's behavior. I was confused. They always bought me new clothes as the old clothes wore out.

One night at the dinner table, Anita said, "Arturo, Julian needs a suit."

"Again?" he cried, "his last suit was for his confirmation."

"He's big now." She made a sewing motion and winked.

"Oh, I see."

I was thoroughly confused but paid no attention and went off to bed.

The next day Anita took me shopping. "Where are you going?" Mr. Costas popped up as we were leaving.

Anita replied, "We're buying Julian a suit; he's a big boy now and he doesn't have one."

"Why does he need a suit?" Mr. Costas asked.

"I need to look good for the ladies," I said.

"Ah, yes. I understand," he mused. "How old are you now?"

With pride, I answered, "I just turned sixteen."

He looked me up and down, scribbled out a pass for us and added, "Be home by four-thirty. Arturo likes his dinner by six sharp."

I laughed and said, "How do you know what my father likes, Mr. Costas?"

"It's my job," he answered, but it wasn't funny. Anita and I walked to the men's clothing store. The shoe shelves were empty, the suit rack was sparse, and instead of three salesmen there was one. He measured me and led me to the racks for my size.

Before I had a chance to even look through the rack, my mother pulled a blue suit off the rack, checked the size of the lapels and the buttons and declared, "We'll take it! Julian, you pay for it."

Later, I asked my father why there weren't any shoes in the store.

"The same reason I have no more crystals for the chandeliers," he said. "Before Castro, the Cuban peso was on par with the American dollar and the dollar was in common circulation. I could order my parts from Austria and Czechoslovakia and pay for them in either currency." I listened intently as the history lesson continued. "One of the first things Castro did was to stop the exchange between the peso and foreign currency at banks. We are no longer permitted to send money overseas because that calls for a conversion. He nationalized all foreign businesses which included major corporations such as the Cuban Sugar Company, the U. S. Fruit Company, the American Telephone and Telegraph Company, Woolworths and many others. His slogan is, when you walk into those stores and companies you are entering free territory—and now instead of music, you have his speeches on the loudspeakers."

Shortly after that, all the TV stations were nationalized, then the radio stations and the newspapers. To this day there is only one political party in Cuba and the papers are published under the auspices of the Communist Party. No free press, no civil liberties, no judicial system; it is a total police state."

At this time, the Cuban peso was worth five pesos to a dollar or twenty cents. Before Castro in 1959 the Cuban peso was equal to the U.S. dollar.

The day after we purchased my suit, my mother ran into the store, Mr. Costas on her heels.

"Arturo," she cried, "My cousin in Spain is deathly ill and not expected to survive the next couple of months. I can't leave now. Can we send Julian to help out? It will only be for a short while." Costas listened intently.

My father comforted her and said, "Don't worry, I will make the arrangements."

I stood on long lines to take pictures for my passport. The next step was to stand on more long lines to get an application for the passport. I filled out the application, which included the reason that I needed to leave the country for a short while to help an ailing and dying relative in Spain. I needed a letter from the police that I had never committed a crime, nor was I involved with any anti-revolutionary groups. With proof of identity (my birth certificate along with additional proof), I received the required shots to travel. I delivered my papers to the passport office with the assurance that I would be notified by mail when the passport would be ready. Although Mr. Costas kept a close eye on me, he loosened the rules a little; a result no doubt of my handshake with Che Guevara. He often referred to my brush with one of history's greatest martyrs and offered to provide a letter stating I was free of any anti-revolutionary activity if it would help speed the process. I thanked him and included it in our papers. My father thanked him personally.

The next step was to secure a visa, which I tried to do through the Mexican and Spanish embassies. I was not successful. My father contacted someone at my old school, still run by priests, and was able to obtain an exit visa from the Spanish Embassy. Once my visa was stamped on my passport, my father got in touch with Uncle Pepe in New York, and asked him to purchase a money order in American dollars and send it by mail to us to purchase an airline ticket for a flight from Havana to Madrid. It took months to accomplish.

The rumors of an invasion intensified. Rafael came to the store one day to speak to my dad. At the end of the conversation, all I heard was, "I'm glad we straightened everything out. I'll take care of the last part of the plan, and then it is goodbye." Two hours later Rafael returned with a career sailor. He was in his mid-forties, balding, wiry, and highly energetic, and with a menacing manner and a wide scowl. Mr. Costas poked his nose into the doorway and said, "Who is this?"

Rafael replied with a wink and a nod "A tourist from Spain. Say hello to Miguel." Mr. Costas nodded, was satisfied, and left.

Arturo, gun in his belt, led the men to his private office. He told me to lock the door and join them. I was shocked but complied immediately. Rafael sat at the edge of the desk. Arturo guided the sailor to the wobbly chair while he and I stood shoulder to shoulder behind the desk in front of the open, empty safe.

Rafael said, "Show him what you have." My father placed three of my mother's lace handkerchiefs filled with jewels and coins on the desk along with my school photo, which surprised me. Miguel placed my photo in his wallet next to a photo of small children, and lifted each handkerchief separately.

"No problem," He said. "I'll pack each one individually and make three separate shipments.

"Why can't you do it in one shipment?" Arturo inquired.

"Too risky," Miguel responded, "I have to spread them out but I will deliver the first one personally."

"How much?" Arturo asked.

"Seven hundred fifty American," Miguel said. Arturo spread out six American one-hundred dollar bills, but Miguel repeated, "Seven hundred fifty."

Six-hundred is all I have, take it or leave it."

Miguel scooped up the six hundred dollars in a flash. He packed the handkerchiefs in his shaving kit at the bottom of his duffel bag and said, "I'll send you details for each pickup."

"How long will it take?" Arturo asked.

"Have him in Manhattan by New Years," was the reply.

"Manhattan, I thought I was going to Spain?"

I was thrilled, frightened and so confused. Crazy thoughts ran through my mind. I wondered if they had green grapes in New York. Was I going to see snow? When would I see my parents again? My stomach hurt.

• • •

I arrived home early from taking pictures. The store was closed but it wasn't Sunday. I ran upstairs, my mother was crying, my father pacing. There was an old antique suitcase from the store in the hallway. As soon as I entered, my father said, "It's time to pack. You're leaving in two hours and remember, don't fall in love with Madrid. We have to get you to New York."

I went to my room, packed quickly then straightened my books, flipped through my stamp collection and straightened my ship and plane models, and smoothed out my bed. My small room had been my haven for my entire life. My possessions were my friends and I loved them dearly. I looked in the mirror one last time, combed my hair and said, "Good-bye my dear friends." I placed my camera around my neck and closed the door forever.

My parents and I went to the airport by taxi. Goodbyes were painful; we traveled in silence. I stared out at the streets, and focused on the hate signs against America on the walls and lamp posts and in windows. We were back at Rancho Boyeros Airport where I first said goodbye to my Aunt Carmen and Uncle Pepe. It was poorly maintained. Armed guards patrolled.

My mother grabbed me and cried; my father gave me a dime and said, "Hide this." I still carry it to this day.

Just then a militia man came up to me and said, "You cannot take that camera out of the country. It is for the revolution."

My father said to him, "Jose, how does your wife like those earrings I gave you?"

The guard said to him, "Ah, Senor, is this kid yours?" My father nodded.

"Where is he going?"

"To Madrid," my father said and the guard issued a pass for me to keep the camera. He then led us to the ticket counter that was under the sign *Flights to Madrid.*

"I'll keep an eye on him," Jose assured us, "by the way, my birthday is coming up."

"Stop by the store and we will celebrate," my father responded. Arturo was fearless, had little respect for people and clearly knew his audience. I stood on line for a while and looked around, mesmerized by all the activity of the small airport. There was a tension in the air. I looked across the aisle and there was Rafael and his family on line under a sign *Flights to Montreal.*

I wondered if my parents knew Rafael was leaving; if they knew he was here at the airport at the same time. He caught my eye. Not an emotion passed between us. He would never know how his behavior with my mother affected me. At that moment, I didn't feel a thing, I was just glad he was going far away from her. The line finally moved; I presented my passport and ticket to the clerk, she stamped them, attached the pass for the camera and sent me back to my seat. More tears, more goodbyes. My father took me aside and placed his arm around me. I whispered, "I'm scared Papa."

He whispered back, "Vargas will meet you at the airport in Madrid. Keep your final destination a secret from these monkeys."

"I will."

"Guard your suit carefully."

"My suit?" I asked incredulously.

"Yes, your suit. Cash and coins are sewed into the lapels, waistband and behind the buttons. Keep it safe, it's for your mother and me. We'll need that to live on when we get out of here. Trust no one. I'll write and send you instructions."

"What?" didn't he know that if I were caught, I could be sent to jail—or worse?" No answer. I was horrified. "When will I see you and Mama again?"

He disentangled himself and answered, "We'll wait here until you board and the plane takes off. Try to wave at your mother." He turned his back.

"Papa, I love you. Papa?" I stood in place, head bowed.

. . .

Passengers' names were called over a loudspeaker. *"Julian Vida!"* My mother jumped up, my father twitched. I quietly gathered my luggage and Jose led me to a room where there was more armed militia. I got on line with the other passengers and one by one, we were searched thoroughly. I almost drowned in sweat. They missed the contraband. My luggage was unpacked and gone through piece by piece. From there we were led to the airstrip. The baggage handler took our luggage from us and gave us ticket stubs. Before boarding, I waved as instructed.

BOOK II

Madrid, Spain

CHAPTER FIVE

April 14, 1961
The Plane

I had never flown before. My life as I knew it was over, I was wholly unprepared for the adventure to come. The plane took off at about 11:30 p.m. I gripped the armrest on takeoff and then relaxed as the plane straightened out. There was a lot of chatter from the passengers who ranged from infancy to elderly folk. I had the window seat, ignored everyone around me, and stared as the lights of Havana dimmed in the dark night, knowing I would never see it again. I tried to relax, but within a short time, the stewardesses seemed upset. There were several trips to the captain's quarters by one particular stewardess and every time she came back to the cabin, she hurried up and down the aisles whispering to the other stewardesses as if she were delivering messages. Clearly something was happening.

The loudspeaker went on and the captain made an announcement which went something like this: *"We've been contacted by the Havana Airport Control Tower and ordered to return to Cuba. Anti-revolutionaries have landed southeast of Havana."* He paused; there was immediate reaction from the passengers, which included crying and shouting, everyone

---

According to Wikipedia, on April 15, 1961, American backed bombers attacked Cuban air fields. The long rumored invasion had begun.

talking at once. He continued, *"My co-pilot, the stewardesses and I have opted to proceed to Madrid and ask for political asylum."* The mood was jubilant. He continued, *"We will refuel in the Azores. Anyone wishing to leave the plane and return to Cuba at that time is free to do so."*

Shouts of "No!" rang out. "On to Madrid," became the mantra. There was great jubilation. Frightened, confused but excited, I sat back and smiled. Let the adventure begin.

I gripped the armrest again. We landed in the Azores in the middle of the night for refueling and were allowed to wander through the terminal until departure. I was fascinated by the array of newspapers, magazines, chocolates and cigarettes available for purchase. My world was growing and I was excited by the view.

Later that day, which was the following day in Madrid, we landed at Barajas Airport. The terminal was a magnificent structure. I stood with my fellow passengers in the immigration line with my old suitcase, and passed the time admiring elegantly dressed people. My fear waned; I was too tired to be frightened, or so I thought. There was a significant presence of the Guardia Civil (Civil Guard) which is a military force charged with police duties. It is an honor to be a member and members are trusted and respected by the populace. Each member of the force is known as *benemérita* (reputable man.) They are responsible for, among other duties, national border patrol and security. Their motto is *El honor es mi divisa* (Honor is my badge).

I wondered where Vargas was, what he looked like. I noticed a calm, dignified man about forty-five dressed in the military uniform of the Guardia Civil approach the clerks and show them papers and a photo. Together, they scanned the line of people. Suddenly, all eyes settled on me. I was trapped and unable to move. A clerk was going through my luggage. The guard flashed his badge and made his way to me, ordered the clerk to stop searching my luggage, and then pulled me aside.

In a loud voice he said, "Julian Vida, come with me." I panicked.

My fellow passengers seemed nervous and I heard rumblings of concern; they thought I was being arrested.

For a moment, so did I until he whispered, "Julian, I'm here to take you to my home."

I answered breathlessly, "Thank you, Vargas!"

My parents neglected to tell me he was in the military, but I was so grateful he was. "Come with me," he demanded. I complied. He flashed his badge again to the clerks as he ushered me out of the building. I was rescued.

"Are my parents alright?" I begged.

"Move quickly, the invasion has begun. It is an international incident. You were on the last flight out of Cuba and all travel has been banned, communications closed down, I need to get you out of here." He took me to a waiting car and we sped through the streets of Madrid to a small, clean, inviting, middle class apartment located in a rural area outside of the city. There was no pavement on the road, just mud that covered my shoes.

April 15, 1961
Vargas Home, Madrid, Spain

Cousin Gracie, thirty-five, plump, pleasant and energetic, welcomed me with open arms and an abundant hug. They were humble, religious people, eager to serve humanity and especially family.

We sat around the kitchen table covered with newspapers. The headlines highlighted the "Bay of Pigs Invasion." I prodded Vargas about calling my parents. Gracie, clearly upset, said she tried calling several times as soon as the news broke, but was unable to get through because the telephone lines were down. They promised they would try again, often, until they got through. I suddenly realized I might never see my parents again and became distraught. Gracie hovered over me trying to console me.

I asked Vargas, "Do you think I will ever see my parents again?"

"I honestly don't know, but for now you are safe."

Gracie flittered about preparing food. "Tell me about your flight, Julian, were you frightened?"

I realized how tired I was—now I was worried as well. With my stomach in knots, food was the last thing I needed.

"Please excuse me, it was a very long flight, may I go to sleep now?"

"Are you sure you're not hungry?"

Before I could answer, Vargas chimed in.

"He's half asleep, let the boy rest. We'll check on him later."

They showed me the bathroom, and then led me to a small, barren room with a cot. I quickly washed, undressed and climbed onto the cot, careful to hang my suit where I could see it. Just as I was about to fall asleep, Gracie and Vargas entered the room.

"Are you sure you're not hungry?" Gracie sweetly asked.

"I think I'm cold," I murmured.

Vargas said, "Of course, the weather here is different than Cuba's weather."

Within a flash, Gracie was covering me with blankets.

"They're heavy. Thank you, thank you so much for everything."

Gracie and Vargas hovered over me as I drifted off to sleep. I heard Gracie say I was a nice gentleman and I liked that.

Then she asked Vargas, "How long do you think he will be with us?"

Vargas mused, "I don't know."

Gracie asked, "Do you think Anita and Arturo will ever get out?"

Vargas replied, "Not any time soon."

That's all I remember until late the next day. I arose half asleep and realized my suit was gone!

I snapped to attention and ran to the kitchen. The coffee smelled good. Gracie was setting up an ironing board. My suit hung on the door.

"Ah, good morning—or should I say good afternoon!" she sang.

"Good day Gracie," I mumbled. I reached for my suit and said, "Please don't trouble yourself."

"No trouble," she hummed. "I'll just freshen this up for you. "She began to steam it and noticed my concern. "Perhaps you would like to do it, I will show you how."

"Yes!" I said too quickly and she guided me with the hot iron. I was careful to barely touch the lapels and avoid the buttons. Did she know?

I slept a lot, Gracie hovered, Vargas went off to work. It was a busy time for the Guardia Civil. I helped Gracie around the house to earn my way and keep busy. I remember folding the laundry—

"Fold in thirds," she instructed, "it gives me more room."

Gracie showed me how to iron without scorching. We spent a lot of time in the kitchen where I read every newspaper I could find for news about the invasion, and tried desperately and unsuccessfully to call my parents. Gracie and I passed the time in between calls to Havana preparing simple meals which she taught me how to cook and serve. I have no idea how many days passed when Vargas came home with mail and shouted excitedly, "Julian, a letter from your folks."

I grabbed it, ripped it open and scanned it quickly. With a sigh of relief and tears in my eyes, I announced, "They're okay. I have to go to the American Embassy!"

I immediately realized I did not have a peseta to my name and I was humiliated. (Spanish currency which, at that time, was sixty pesetas and was equal to one dollar.)

I sobbed, "I have no money! How will I repay you?"

Vargas responded, "Your father took care of it, relax. We'll get you there, boy."

Vargas sketched out a map while Gracie counted out six-hundred pesetas equal to about ten dollars. I was eager to leave the house and see Madrid. How long would six-hundred pesetas last?

With Vargas' crudely drawn map in hand, I took deep breaths and ventured out on my own with great courage, a bit of anxiety and an eagerness to roam free. I took a bus to the train station. That cost two pesetas. I had never been on a train or in a subway. I needed the subway to get to the center of Madrid. That cost another two pesetas. It was a frightening, and at the same time, an exhilarating adventure. With ease I located the United States Embassy.

May, 1961
U.S. Embassy, Madrid, Spain

The energy was intoxicating; sounds bounced off the walls. A teletype machine ran constantly grinding out wide sheets of paper that fell into a basket. There were rows of clerks behind open cubicles providing information and guidance to what seemed like dozens of people of every race, age and economic status, moving briskly from line to line. So many people wanted to go to America. I prayed I'd be accepted.

As I stood on the information line, from what I could gather, there were at least three situations why people wanted to get to America:

- Travel for business or pleasure,
- Establishing a business,
- Seeking residency.

I sought permanent residency and was given a packet of forms to complete along with several pages of instructions. It was overwhelming so I took the packet, found a quiet area, and sat at a counter to read the forms. As best as I can remember, the packet contained:

- An application for permanent residency which included my name, contact number, education, history of work, physical description and whether or not I was a member of the Communist Party. That impressed me and it pleased me to make a large, dark check mark in the **NO** box.

- A form for contact information for the person or persons who were to sponsor me in the United States. That was easy, Uncle Pepe in New York. I had to attach the following copies:

- Uncle Pepe's bank Statement(s).

- A notarized letter of employment from Uncle Pepe's place of work.

- A copy of his lease or proof of home ownership.

- A notarized letter confirming his ability and willingness to take responsibility for me so that I would not become a public nuisance. That offended me.

- A list of local doctors in Madrid and I had to have a full physical.

- A letter from the doctor describing my overall health.

- Proof of appropriate vaccinations.

- Copy of blood work.

- Lung x-ray with written report.

- Photocopy of my passport.

Clearly there was a lot to do. I needed to walk to clear my head, so I walked and walked through the streets of Madrid. Madrid was simply beautiful. The architecture was mesmerizing; the store windows, filled with upscale clothing, jewelry, and furniture drew me in, for the items on display were like a window to another world of which I vowed to be a part. Ambition circled my mind and embraced my soul. People were elegantly dressed and well mannered, friendly and courteous. No one lingered in doorways, ogled women or made snide remarks. There was an air of respectability, and eventually, I felt at home.

As I walked I tried to figure out how I was going to pay for the doctor's fees, the lab fees, x-ray fees and the visa fees. I also needed money for the airline ticket to fly to America. I was not allowed to touch the money in the suit, nor was it feasible for me to take a job in Madrid. I had no skills, couldn't commit to time, and my father did not want me to complicate *The Plan*. I remembered his words, "Don't fall in love with Madrid."

I wrote to him to describe my needs and told him to mail as much of my stamp collection as he could. I wrote to my uncle Pepe and sent him all the forms requiring his input. And then I waited.

My focus every day was on receiving mail. At great personal risk, my father worked through the black market to send what money and possessions he could to me for safekeeping in America. If he were caught, it would have meant imprisonment, or worse. Most of his money and possessions found their way as promised, although there were a couple of cheaters in the mix who basically stole his money and ran.

• • •

Arturo and Anita wrote as often as they could and sent money wrapped in letters and photos. Within each letter there was also a page or two of Arturo's legal documents, which included the titles to the apartment building he owned, and the building which housed his antique business and our town home above it. I also received my birth certificate and graduation certificate from the Bi-Lingual Business Academy in Havana.

Arturo paid five to one, or a hundred pesos for twenty dollars, so within a couple of weeks, twenty dollar money orders arrived. I accumulated enough to pay for some of the services I needed, but it wasn't enough for carfare, lunch and incidentals. I was worried.

I chose a doctor from the list provided by the embassy and had a thorough examination. I had the required blood tests, lung x-ray and vaccinations. The doctor gave me a letter indicating my overall health was good.

Within a few weeks, Uncle Pepe returned all the forms required along with a letter explaining how sorry he was, but that he really couldn't support me financially and I would have to find a job immediately upon arrival in New York. I wasn't trained in any trade, nor was I educated in any profession. What was I supposed to do? I'd figure it out. I focused on Arturo's *Plan*. I wrote back to Uncle Pepe and assured him I would get a job as soon as possible.

I had to get to New York. My papers were in order so my plan was to rise early the next day and arrive at the American Embassy when it opened, so I could be first in line. I slept well.

• • •

June, 1961
Madrid, Spain

I rose early, took the bus to the train, and the train to Madrid. It was rush hour and crowded so I was crammed up against a pole in very close proximity to a very attractive woman. Clutching my papers in one hand, holding onto the pole with the other, between the rocking motion of the train and her intoxicating perfume, I am afraid, my manhood made an inconvenient appearance. It was too crowded for me to faint, and I felt my blood rushing through my body and settled in my face, so I stood as red as a beet and stared straight ahead hoping and praying that Junior would go back to sleep and the woman wouldn't scream for help. On the contrary, when the train stopped, I dashed for the door.

She hooked her arm through mine and cooed, "That was the nicest compliment I received all week." I mumbled an apology and asked for forgiveness."

She looked me up and down and whispered. "Too bad, I like my men older, slower and very rich. Are you very rich?" I hesitated. She answered for me, "Of course not, you're just a kid. Well, I had fun. Have a nice day."

In retrospect, I had fun too. I gathered my thoughts and focused on the task at hand. I arrived at the U.S. Embassy and handed in my completed packet with great pride. The clerk reviewed all my papers to make sure all were in order; he date stamped them and placed my packet along with dozens of other applications in a designation bin. He gave me an appointment to return in six weeks. He then guided me to a section where I was fingerprinted and my photo was taken.

During a rare phone call, my father told me my cousin Miguel (the sailor who took my father's jewels to New York) was marrying a girl named Elizabeth who gained weight and looked as big as a whale. I understood that was the name of a ship. He told me she recently moved to New Jersey, close to Manhattan and was expecting a baby by New Years. That was my first coded message to pick up the first of three scheduled, knotted handkerchiefs filled with jewelry and coins. I had no information about the other two at that time. All I knew was that I had to be in New York to claim my family's jewels by December thirty-first. I had a few months, but first, I had to learn where New Jersey was.

Most days after lunch, I put on my suit, my freshly washed and ironed shirt, added two tee-shirts to keep warm, and made the trip to the center of Madrid. After stopping at the U.S. Embassy to check on my paperwork a few times, I was told I just had to be patient. There was nothing anyone could do to speed up the process. That signaled to me to stop checking in so often; I did not want to incur their wrath. I waited for all the paperwork to be processed. And I waited.

I walked everywhere, exploring the shops and restaurants, finding new streets which led to interesting buildings. I spent a lot of my time visiting book stores, called Librerias, and read as much as I could about New York. I found New Jersey and its port closest to Manhattan. I had one role of film, thirty-six pictures, so I economically chose my sites for photos. Rather than spend money developing the role, I just packed it away for future memories.

I went to the park, El Retiro, and sat by the lake for hours. The birds and gardens calmed me, but when I saw couples walking hand in hand I felt sad. I visited the Palacio Real museum where the king used to live. I visited the Prado museum and other museums, and all the touristy places my limited funds would allow. I walked the Grande Via, and Calle de Alcala, which housed upscale shops and restaurants.

The theaters were magnificent. I went to the movies twice, at a cost of about sixty pesetas. I purchased my ticket and was shown a map of the theater for a reserved seat that I chose, and was guided to the seat by an usher. The movie was *Ben Hur*; what a spectacle! It was quite a memorable experience. A couple of weeks later I saw *Psycho,* it made me nervous. It was much different than my experience in Cuba. I also saw an Agatha Christie play and to this day, have great respect for live theater.

The food was wonderful. I discovered tapas and treated myself to a beer—once! Individual cigarettes were available for one peseta. I smoked and felt quite sophisticated. I never went to a bullfight, it was simply too expensive.

In Madrid I was most impressed with the glamour and elegance of the women, the manners and respectability of the men, the clean streets. Had circumstances been different for me, I would have been happy to make Madrid my home.

My stamp collection arrived. I visited a stamp house in Madrid where the owner, a small, round man with large eye glasses and a cool detached manner, sifted through my stamp collection. I watched him carefully and noticed his eyes widen when he came upon a Zeppelin stamp from the United States.

"You have a good eye," he nonchalantly remarked. Then too quickly, said, "How about a trade?"

I remembered my father's lesson and said, "Let's discuss a price first; cash only."

But then he said, "I'm only interested in a portion of the collection. How much discount do you offer for a portion?"

"None, my prices are firm."

Arturo would have been proud. I tripled my investment and received full price. His interest spurred mine and after doing some additional research at a book store, I raised my prices for the next sale.

Now I had enough money to buy an airline ticket to the United States. I was thrilled at the prospect of going to New York but I was under pressure from my parents. My father's business was drying up; my parents were miserable; I had to get them out of Havana!

Vargas and Gracie were kind and gracious but I knew they were eager for me to reunite with my family. The six weeks passed and it was time for my appointment.

• • •

July, 1961
U.S. Embassy, Madrid, Spain

My appointment day arrived. There was great anticipation and anxiety. I freshened up my suit and tie, put on a newly washed and ironed shirt, and off I went to the Embassy.

The American consul, who spoke Spanish, interviewed me for over an hour. After determining that all papers were in order, he asked me if I was going to school. I showed him my graduation certificate from the Havana Business Academy. He put it aside and advised me that since I was a minor I would have to go to school in America and earn a high school equivalency diploma. He asked about my English skills. I spoke broken English like a tourist, so he suggested I study English and become more proficient.

We talked about Cuba and the hope that my parents were going to join me in the United States. He was sympathetic and issued permanent residence status with the understanding and obligation that every January first I was to report my address to the Department of Immigration and Naturalization Service, using a postcard form I was to obtain from the post office. To apply for citizenship, I had to wait five years. We shook hands and I left. I wandered the streets for a while with the sinking feeling that I might never see Madrid again.

I went to the book store and read again, everything I could about Manhattan. I was thrilled and had a warm sense of freedom. I bought a bouquet of flowers for Gracie and Vargas.

CHAPTER SIX

July, 1961
Vargas Apartment, Madrid, Spain

Entering the apartment with celebration in my heart, I was stunned by the enormous octopus wrapped around the hot and cold faucets in the kitchen sink.

"We're celebrating," Gracie squealed, "today is our third anniversary in this apartment!"

"Congratulations!" I responded, "and today I received my entry visa to the United States and my application for permanent residency was approved. I'm going to New York!"

"Wonderful," said Vargas, "tonight we celebrate! Gracie is preparing her specialty, octopus and rice!" The conversation was lively, the wine was sweet, the octopus was chewy. I was constipated for days.

The next day I entered the Pan American Airlines office and requested the least expensive one way ticket to New York. A very nice lady checked my papers, noted that I was from Cuba, and asked me if I was traveling alone. I told her I was and that I hoped to bring my parents out of Cuba as soon as possible. She excused herself and asked me to wait at her desk. Had I said too much? I heard my father deep down in my gut, "Don't trust anyone!"

Too late, she returned with a priest. I was confused. She introduced me to Father Joseph. I stood, bowed slightly, and shook his hand gently. He patted me on the back and asked me when I had attended church last. I told him of my early education and that I hadn't been to church since then.

He smiled broadly. "He will do," and then he disappeared.

That lovely lady arranged for me to travel with the priest and his group of seminary students. It appeared they had an extra seat in their group and if I could leave within three days I would be given a significantly reduced rate as part of the group. I was grateful.

· · ·

July, 1961
Barajas Airport, Madrid, Spain

Gracie, Vargas and I embraced. They were simply loving and kind people to whom I was forever grateful. With tears in our eyes, we said our goodbyes.

"I will miss you, thank you doesn't seem enough," I said from the heart.

Gracie said, "Just make a smile for me and that will be enough."

Vargas placed his arm around me and said, "A couple of months ago, I picked up a boy. Now I say good-bye to a man."

"We are proud of you," Gracie added.

My boarding announcement came over the loudspeaker. We grabbed last hugs and said our good-byes. Sadly, I never saw them again, nor did I ever return to Spain.

I lined up with Father Joseph and twenty-four seminary students at the departure gate. We entered the plane and again I had a window seat. I crossed my legs and noticed the holes in my shoes. How was I going to pay for a new pair of shoes? I leaned back, shut my eyes and thought, "Let the adventure begin."

BOOK III

New York City, New York

CHAPTER SEVEN

JULY, 1961
IDLEWILDE AIRPORT, NEW YORK

It had been three years since we said good-bye to Aunt Carmen and Uncle Pepe at the Havana airport. I was excited to reconnect with them and joyfully embraced them. Pepe and Carmen responded with restraint. I stared at Uncle Pepe, remembering our last conversation at my thirteenth birthday party.

"I didn't realize how much you look like Papa," Pepe replied, "Yes, yes, let's get out of here—I don't like crowds." Aunt Carmen admired my suit, felt the lapels.

"Nice suit, Julian, well-made."

"Thank you, Tia." (Aunt).

I remembered thinking she is a pattern maker and seamstress, so maybe she was just admiring the work. Did she know what was sewn in? I was disappointed at the underwhelming welcome, grabbed my suitcase and trotted behind Aunt Carmen and Uncle Pepe.

During the taxi ride, I attempted to make conversation.

"Aunt Carmen, remember at my party you told me all about Manhattan, and the Statue of Liberty, and the United Nations building. I want to see everything!"

Aunt Carmen said quietly, "Tomorrow, Julian, tomorrow we will take you sightseeing. Let's get you settled."

The light was gone from her eyes; there was no enthusiasm, no fun. They changed. It made me sad, and as I stared out of the window of the taxi, I was mesmerized by the heights of the buildings and the amount of apartment houses.

We arrived in the Spanish Harlem section of Manhattan. It was hot and humid; windows were open, doors were ajar, bongo sounds reverberated through the air, as did loud chatter. People of all ages loitered in doorways, on corners, on fire escapes, and rooftops. The energy was happy, electric. I didn't understand the language. It wasn't Castilian Spanish, but a mixture of Puerto Rican Spanish and English. I missed Madrid.

I looked up at the six-story pre-war building, the entrance covered by a green awning with the address imprinted on both sides. The one-bedroom, one bathroom apartment, with a sunken living room, had high ceilings and several windows. It was sparsely, inexpensively furnished. The dining room set was Formica—the chairs were metal with cheap cushions. The bedroom set was secondhand and badly scratched. The living room contained an old used couch with duct tape repairs. There were two mismatched chairs to the side and across the way. Under the window was a two door cabinet that had a broken door and a small T.V. on top.

"You'll sleep here on the couch," my aunt announced, "put your clothes in the cabinet."

I thought I detected a bit of embarrassment. From my uncle I felt annoyance.

I thought my aunt and uncle had been gone long enough to have better than just old, badly used furniture. Clearly they were struggling economically and they did not seem as happy together as they did in Havana. I wondered what went wrong. As I placed my suitcase alongside the couch, my aunt and uncle hung a sheet in the living room, to one side of the couch, for their privacy.

I settled in on the bumpy couch for my first night in New York. I focused on tomorrow and sightseeing—and getting outside of the neighborhood.

After a quick shower, abbreviated breakfast of buttered French bread and coffee, the three of us left early in the morning and spent the day on buses exploring Manhattan. I kept all the maps and made note of the streets and avenues. Aunt Carmen chattered non-stop explaining the sights. I had the feeling they did not get out much. Uncle Pepe was reserved but seemed to enjoy himself; it was hard to tell, but the grimace was gone, so I assumed that was his happy face.

We started at the Statue of Liberty—magnificent! We walked through Chinatown, Little Italy and Greenwich Village. Aunt Carmen remembered that I never saw snow so she bought me a snow filled glass souvenir. We visited the Empire State building and rode the elevator to the top. We passed Macy's, advertised as *The World's Largest Store* and ate lunch at a Chock Full O'

Nuts coffee shop where they had counter service only; no tipping allowed. I ate creamed cheese on raisin walnut bread. Delicious.

Our last stop was the United Nations building and the gift shop where they sold stamps of the world. I made note to return so I could buy stamps to rebuild my collection.

We returned home, exhausted and happy. I asked a thousand questions that Aunt Carmen answered as best she could. I was excited to see Manhattan and feel its energy. Uncle Pepe suggested we take a nap before dinner. He had things to discuss with me later. Uh, oh, that did not sound good.

I spread out on the couch, shook my souvenir, and as I watched the snow fall in the glass ball I drifted off to sleep. I was awakened by a man talking in English about the weather. It was the T.V.! Uncle Pepe decided to read the newspaper and watch the T.V. news while Aunt Carmen prepared her famous dry chicken limbs dinner, served with white rice. Dessert was ice cream. Uncle Pepe loved chocolate swirl; fruit was too expensive. No fruit!

During the time I lived with my aunt and uncle, I learned to sleep with the T.V. running. The sheet offered little privacy while my aunt and uncle watched T.V. every night and I slept on the couch.

Then there was the mystery of the American chicken. More than once a week, my aunt prepared chicken wings and legs for dinner, either with white rice, or powdered mashed potatoes mixed with milk. I honestly thought there were no complete chickens in America. To this day I will not eat a wing or a leg; I am strictly a chicken breast man. But what I remember most from those days is the smell of hot dogs—I didn't have enough money to buy one.

When dinner was over, my aunt disappeared and my uncle began *the* conversation. "You don't think you are going to live here for free, do you Julian?"

"No! Of course not! Didn't my father send you money?" I was embarrassed and confused.

"Not enough to support a teenage boy in my house!" he roared.

"I have some money left over from the sale of my stamp collection but I need to use that for my expenses and to bring my parents out of Cuba. Look at my shoes, Tio (uncle)."

"How much do you have?" he inquired.

"Two hundred dollars," I replied.

I'll take a hundred and you will get a job and earn your keep. You will help your aunt with the chores around here, right boy?"

"Right," I agreed. He waited while I removed a hundred dollars from my wallet and gave it to him.

He counted it twice and said, "I'm not as generous as your father. I don't agree we have to feed family!" He was clearly angry at the situation. "Find a job and make it quick!"

He threw the newspaper at me and stormed off to bed.

I didn't sleep well that night. I read the paper as best I could from front to back. It was *The New York Times*. I found the employment section and scanned the listings. I wasn't trained or educated, so what was I supposed to do, for what kind of a job would I qualify?

I found an ad that read B. Altman & Co., stock boy needed. I knew the word stock from my father's store. I assumed it meant the same thing. I needed to speak to my father.

The next day, I was awakened by a slammed door. Uncle Pepe went off to work. I dressed quickly, folded the sheet, straightened the couch and went to the kitchen to help Aunt Carmen.

"Sit down Julian. I want you to understand what has happened."

I obeyed. "Your uncle works very hard, as do I, but the pay here is little and money is tight. Your father was right, Pepe's business failed and he works for someone else. Don't tell your father, Pepe is too proud. Now we can't go home to Havana. There's no home to go to, so he is angry and sad and mad. We don't laugh anymore. He just lies around like potato salad. He won't have sex with me anymore."

"Tia, please. I don't want to hear that."

"What's the difference," she replied, "we're family."

"Aunt Carmen, I am sorry and understand why Uncle Pepe is so angry. I need to get a job. Where is B. Altman? I saw in the newspaper that they need a stock boy."

Aunt Carmen looked in the telephone book.

I excused myself, dressed quickly, took the paper and the written instructions from Aunt Carmen, and off I went downtown by subway—on the A train. The New York subway was more efficient and faster than the one in Madrid, but more crowded and less clean. And there I was right across the street from the magnificent Empire State building! With the ad, my passport and graduation certificate from the Havana Business Academy in hand, I entered the large, beautiful department store, was directed to the personnel department, took my first test in English, passed and was hired on the spot. I was given a quick tour of the store, which included a cafeteria for employees. I was proud and excited about my first job in wonderful Manhattan. I was told I had to wear a shirt and tie, was assigned a locker, and was given a grey smock. I loved the location, the buildings, the restaurants and the energy in the air, with the people rushing to and fro. I took time to walk around the area before I went home to report my success. I would be very happy coming to work every day.

I went home ecstatic and proud, but eager to speak to my parents. Little did I know that my father was going to call that evening.

"Papa," I squealed with delight, "how are you, how is Mama? I miss you, are you okay? I have so much to tell you."

Sternly he replied, "Now is not the time. I don't know where your cousin Miguel is staying. I hope I hear from him soon, otherwise I got fucked!"

"Don't worry, Papa. I got a job in a big store. I will take care of you and Mama. Manhattan is wonderful. The buildings are so high, the streets are so wide. So many people, so beautiful, you will love it here." CLICK. He hung up.

Uncle Pepe asked what my salary was to be. If memory serves I earned fifty dollars a week. Uncle Pepe demanded twenty so after taxes, that left me with approximately fifteen dollars for carfare and lunch. Entertainment, clothes—not yet; I wasn't prepared for the weather changes to come, and I still needed a pair of shoes.

My first day at work I was sent to the linen department where towels arrived rolled in packages of forty-eight. The heavy rolls had to be off loaded from the delivery truck, loaded into a bin, and transported to the stock room of the linen department where they were stacked on high shelves. The work was hard. I noticed that every time I stacked a new batch of towels they got moved or were mixed up and not with their original vendor. The patterns were supposed to match. Every day, I was doing double work. I remembered how my father organized the patterns of crystal he sold for chandeliers—by draping a sample over a box and placing the supply boxes behind each pattern. I went to the shoe department, took empty boxes, cut them to fit the shelves and draped a sample of the towel pattern that was supposed to be in place for every vendor, and made sure the matching towels were in their proper place behind each sample. The salespeople were grateful. It made their jobs easier and it made the stock boys' jobs easier. Everyone was happy except the buyer who should have thought of it. He had me transferred to the high end gifts department where they sold Waterford crystal, vases and other expensive glassware. They were heavier than the towels and more costly. But having grown up around such pieces, I was confident and careful.

In August, shortly after I started work, I was called to the personnel office.

The lady who hired me said, "Because you are only sixteen, you will have to register for school, earn an equivalency diploma and fill out working papers which will have to be signed by your guardian."

"But I have my diploma," I argued.

"That is unacceptable," she retorted. I complied.

By September, I registered for school at night and took the required classes. Frankly, I was glad to be out of the apartment, but a bit intimidated by my classmates. They were a rough crowd; felons, petty criminals, etc. No one bothered me, but I was always aware of my surroundings.

Before heading home on my school nights, if I had enough money, I stopped at a drugstore where I bought some cigarettes and *The New York Times*, a most respected newspaper, which helped me greatly with my study of English. There was a friendly clerk named Stanley. He was a male nurse by trade, and filled in as a clerk in-between private cases. We talked often about current events. He too was a stamp collector, and introduced stamp collecting to his two children. He lived in Brooklyn but loved and knew the city well, so I peppered him with questions about bus and train routes, interesting sights, etc. He let me linger and read magazines without purchasing them, and told me where the local library was. He reminded me of Benjamin, and visiting Stanley gave me the feeling of visiting the bakery in Havana— comfort and trust.

. . .

SEPTEMBER, 1961
NEW YORK CITY, NY

I received a letter from my father informing me that my Cousin Miguel was arriving on the ship LaQuinta, in Hoboken, and wanted to see me September twenty-second at five a.m., which was in four days. This was code for me to pick up the first of my father's three packages, folded in my mother's lace handkerchiefs, which were given to the sailor Miguel Sato before I had left for Madrid. The name of the ship had changed from Elizabeth to LaQuinta, as did the expected date. Pepe and Carmen knew about my father's arrangements and did not approve. They felt he was placing me in danger—which he was. Carmen suggested we all go.

"No, my instructions are to go alone."

"I don't like this smuggling business," she offered.

"It's not smuggling if you are picking up your own family jewels," I responded, and I truly believed that, and knew I did nothing wrong or illegal. I also had to prove to my father that I could save the family jewels. I'd do anything to please my father.

That night after school, I asked Stanley how to get to the docks in Hoboken by five in the morning—on a weekday. Without judgment or questions, he gave me a map that they sold for a dollar twenty-five and showed me the train route. As I left, I saw him place the dollar twenty-five in the cash register from his own pocket; a simple act of kindness.

On Friday, the morning of the first pick-up, (there were to be three in total,) I arose at three a.m., dressed for work in my suit, wrapped a razor in a metal box used for aspirin, followed Stanley's instructions, and arrived in Hoboken at the docks at four forty-five. No one told me the United States Coast Guard was in charge. I was terrified as I approached the coast guard station at the entrance to the dock. A uniformed coast guardsman stepped out of the booth, clipboard in hand.

"How can I help you boy?" he asked.

"I came to see my cousin Miguel Sato, on the ship LaQuinta."

He looked me up and down, then pointed to a ship and waived me through. "There on the right," he coaxed.

I followed his instructions and was stopped by the ship's security guard. Another uniformed man with a clipboard.

"Who are you here to see," he demanded?"

"My cousin, Miguel Sato," I meekly replied. The security guard walked closer to the ship and yelled his name.

"Sato! Miguel Sato! Visitor!"

Miguel came forward and down the ramp. We embraced.

I whispered, "Arturo Vida sends his regards."

Miguel led me out of sight of the guard, who took no notice. Miguel quickly lifted his shirt and removed a taped package from his chest. He handed it to me swiftly along with an envelope he pulled from somewhere else on his body. He worked so fast, I had a hard time keeping up. I secured everything inside my suit pockets.

Miguel whispered, "Here is the first package. The bank statement is in the envelope."

"When and where do I pick up the other two packages," I inquired?

"When your father sends you instructions, now get out of here!" Miguel gave me a final hug and a hardy slap on the back for the benefit of the guard, and headed back towards the ship. I waived at them both and walked quickly off the dock, making sure to acknowledge the coast guardsman as well.

By seven in the morning I was in a noisy coffee shop in Manhattan. I hardly ate my breakfast. I locked my suit jacket with the package and the bank statement in my locker, put on my gray smock and worked all morning lugging heavy glassware to and from the loading docks. It was payday, I studied it, and asked one of my co-workers for an explanation of all the deductions. I told the supervisor I had to go to the bank to open an account, and asked her for the nearest branch of the same bank that was listed on the statement Miguel gave me. She gave me the information and directions. I asked for a few minutes extra. No problem.

At the bank, I asked to see an officer. I explained that my father had an account in the bank and I wished to open my own savings account. He was happy for the business. I also said I needed a safe deposit box; no problem. He showed me to a private room. I was relieved to finally place the package in the box, safe and sound. I never opened the package. I removed my jacket and with the hidden razor blade, slit the lapels. There was one thousand dollars in each lapel which I carefully removed and placed in the box. I removed my pants and carefully slit the waistband which held an additional three thousand dollars. I undid the material covering the buttons on the jacket and the sleeves. The two jacket buttons contained five peso gold coins. The three buttons on each sleeve contained one peso gold coins.

I returned to work, tired but relieved. I needed to work overtime to earn more money. Because I worked six days a week and late on Thursday nights, I met a lot of young people in the department, some full-time employees, some part-time; they were pleasant enough, but I kept to myself.

· · ·

Toward the end of the day, I noticed some of the stock boys and sales girls whispering in the corner. Attention was directed towards me and I was uneasy. Finally, one of the guys approached me and invited me to a party and said, "TGIF". I asked what that meant and he explained, "Thank God it's Friday, we got paid and now we get laid." I called my aunt, told her I was going out with some friends and would be home late. She was indifferent.

We went en-masse by train to an apartment in Greenwich Village where one of the girls lived alone. The apartment, decorated with paper-mache and with beads for doors, vibrated with loud rock music and laughter. I was invited to sit on a floor pillow and given a beer.

Someone shouted, "Thank God it's Friday! Let the party begin!"

One of the guys plopped down next to me and said, "You know the party goes through the weekend."

"You mean I can stay here?" I inquired.

"Do whatever you want. Just remember Saturday is our busiest day!"

Two female hippies stood over us and gyrated to the music. They slithered into our laps and there was a lot of kissing and blind fondling.

The guy whispered, "This is a wild bunch of girls, go slow."

The girls pulled us up to dance. Somehow I wound up behind the beads and in front of my first naked woman. I was frightened, embarrassed and excited all at once. She noticed my bulge and removed a condom from her pocketbook.

"Here," she said, "let's not waste time. Put this on."

I hadn't a clue what she was talking about but figured I would go along with it.

"Why don't you do it?" I was so suave.

She gently undressed me, and put it on me, and proceeded to introduce me to my manhood. The explosion was glorious and I knew I wanted more. By the third time, I mastered it myself. I will forever be thankful to her because she told me you couldn't have sex without it, and I took that advice as gospel. It was good advice. Now I had to figure out how to make the condom purchases part of my meager budget.

What a day, what a night! I don't know how I made it to work the next day. I slept most of Sunday and asked Carmen to help me repair my suit. She never asked how much I had carried from Havana and I was grateful.

· · ·

NOVEMBER, 1961
NEW YORK CITY, NY

A letter arrived with information about the second pick-up of the family jewels.

"Where do you have to go this time?" Pepe inquired.

The next night after school, I asked Stanley how to get to Mott Street, in Chinatown. As always, his directions were perfect. I awoke the following morning at five-thirty and saw my first snowfall. I thought it was beautiful and was eager to walk in it. By seven I was in the cellar of a restaurant, following a lithe middle aged Chinese man, around and through narrow aisles, with wooden shelves, filled with food supplies. Several sacks of soy flour were piled on top of each other and practically reached the low ceiling. I stood aside as he scrambled atop the soy flour sacks, and with his bare hands he reached around the top sack and removed a package.

"I found it," he yelled with glee.

He tossed the package to me and clambered back down from the sacks. I thanked him.

He pushed me towards the exit and said, "Go now, fast please."

I dusted the flour off my suit and rushed to work.

• • •

JANUARY, 1962
NEW YORK CITY APARTMENT

As required by immigration law to register every January, I went to the post office, filled out my address card as a permanent resident alien—and did so every January until I became a citizen. Work was okay, school was going well, and I continued to party. Just as my seventeenth birthday passed I received word that the third package had been delivered and I had to pick it up. This time it was in a penthouse apartment. For the first time I felt safe making the pickup. After all it was on Park Avenue, so I assumed the last pickup for my father would be the easiest.

The lobby of the apartment house was vast and elegant so that I thought it a privilege to be there; I was impressed by the wealth. A doorman checked my name against a list and informed me I was expected. He directed me to a private elevator which went directly to the penthouse. A maid met me at the elevator.

She curtsied and said, "Madame will be with you shortly," and led me into a grand sitting room.

It was going to be a breeze, I thought to myself.

"Please have a seat," she replied.

I sat in an elegant Louis XIV chair surrounded by exquisite artwork and expensive furnishings. I heard a child's giggles as I sat and admired the artwork on the walls.

A young boy hid behind my chair and said, "I bet you can't find me."

"Come out before we both get into trouble," I said.

He stayed where he was and giggled. The maid returned with a tray of tea and cookies and placed it on the table next to me where I sat. She stood at attention while Madame, an elderly sophisticated woman slithered into the room and sat across from me. She was well coiffed, overly made-up, and dressed in a long silky gown, and with jewelry on her ears, wrists, fingers and around her neck; good jewelry, diamonds and pearls, and she wore her glasses around her neck on a gold chain. I immediately stood up to greet her. She pressed her finger to her lips for silence, she looked me over and didn't say a word; nor did I. The maid served Madame a cup of tea and stood aside. Madame was not happy.

"Never mix my tea with our company's tray."

"I'm sorry Madame, it won't happen again."

I sat down. Madame looked at me but addressed the maid. "You are forgiven, you're still new here. Now go pick up my dry cleaning."

"Yes, Ma'am, right away."

She exited. I stood again and started to approach Madame.

"Sit boy, I am not ready for you yet!"

She was rude. I was overwhelmed, annoyed, but I obeyed. Strange group these smugglers. The little boy jumped out from behind my chair and screamed.

"Boo, grandma!"

Madame feigned surprise and fibbed, "Oh you frightened me! Come here and give grandma a hug."

I was getting impatient and not enjoying the show. Madame asked the boy, "Do you love me?"

The boy answered, "I love you grandma. Will you take me to the zoo?"

She answered, "No dear, grandma is busy; stay quiet now."

The boy returned to where I sat and curled up by my feet.

"Okay," he whimpered.

Madame removed an open package from the drawer of a table and placed it on top. I went over to the package and asked why it was open.

Madame answered, "The little one got to it before I realized what he did, so sorry."

I attempted to take it. She caught my hand and claimed, "There's nothing missing, dear. Sit down."

I reluctantly obeyed but never lost sight of my father's package. Madame untied my mother's handkerchief and burrowed through the jewels and coins.

She picked up the coins and said, "I'll keep these."

I was horrified and shouted, "You can't do that!"

"Silly boy, I'll pay you the going rate, thirty-five dollars per ounce."

I stood tall and said, "They are not mine to sell."

The young boy grabbed my leg, but I never took my eyes off the package.

"Think of what you can do with that unreported cash," she implored.

"My parents would never forgive me."

"Mmm, honest and loyal," she purred, "I like you. Work for me as a courier; it pays very well."

"I have a job, Please give me my package, I have to get to work!"

She slapped the table, I was startled.

"No!" she cried, "my grandson should have these coins."

"He won't," I retorted, "they belong to my father!"

The child clung to my leg. I ignored him.

Madame stated, "You're out of your element dear. Tell your father the package was lost. You know the way out!"

Every fiber in my body wanted to smack her. Every lesson I was taught prevented me from doing so. Instead I begged, "He'll kill me!"

"Oh well" she nonchalantly sang, "close the door on the way out!"

I was at a momentary loss.

As she dismissed me with her hand, I picked up the child and said, "Let's go to the zoo!"

Madame screamed, "Put him down!"

"My package," I said.

"No!" She responded.

"What's the going rate on the street for little boys?" I inquired still holding him in my arms.

"You are not as innocent as you appear." She seemed nervous. I felt stronger as the power shifted.

"I grew up with a very shrewd man," I stated.

"How dare you!" she seethed.

"How dare *you* Madame!" I had enough.

With the child in my arms, I headed towards the door. I watched as she grabbed the package and sealed it as best she could. I stopped at the door. She moved toward me, package in hand; a standoff.

"Give me my grandson," she begged.

"Let's trade your family jewel for my family jewels or you will never hear him say 'I love you grandma' again."

The little boy piped up, "I wanna go to the zoo."

"Yes. I'll take you," I volunteered. I opened the door.

"Put him down!" she screamed.

"Hand me the package. I'll leave him outside the door."

Madame forced the package into my hand and grabbed for the child.

I placed the child on the ground and made a hasty exit. Madame grabbed the child, hugged him tight and through her sobs, begged, "Tell grandma you love her." As the elevator door closed, I heard him say "I love you grandma." I was sick to my stomach.

• • •

That night over Carmen's dry chicken parts dinner, I told her and Pepe the story. They were upset.

Carmen said to Pepe, "Do you see what an animal this beautiful boy is turning into? Speak to Arturo."

Pepe took my side.

"She had him against the wall; he had to do something. You know he wouldn't hurt anyone, it's not in him."

Then to change the subject and ease the tension he slapped me on the back and said, "He's becoming quite the lover. Look at all the girls calling him, Give him his messages." so Carmen reluctantly handed me scraps of paper with names and numbers on them.

"I'm not your secretary," she said.

Pepe winked at me, "Go ahead, return your calls."

I scanned the messages; no one important at the moment. Still, I was upset from my encounter and put the messages aside.

With head in hand, I added, "I always associated the wealthy with class and dignity. Boy was I wrong."

Pepe was the calm one this time, "Forget about it. No one got hurt."

Carmen wasn't finished. "Don't be so sure. Damn your brother!"

I then added, "Thank god this was the last pick up. Why can't I just be left alone?"

They took me literally and for the first time since I arrived, they went out after dinner and left me alone. I went to bed early, exhausted and unnerved. Had I turned into an animal? It was time for a Cary Grant movie.

• • •

FEBRUARY 1962
SPANISH HARLEM, NY

Relations between Cuba and the United States were severed. Travel to the United States from Cuba was forbidden; the only way my parents could leave was with permission and a tourist visa to another country. For them to continue to the United States, they needed to go through the same process as I did. Pepe agreed to sponsor them. They needed letters of employment because they were adult; and Aunt Carmen, Uncle Pepe and I discussed it endlessly. We were all trying desperately to reach friends and relatives in other parts of the world to sponsor them. We knew so few people. We were unsuccessful. My parents were miserable and trapped, and unable to communicate with anyone for fear of being punished. Most of their neighbors had fled; some just disappeared. Food was being rationed. My father began to sell everything he could and replaced nothing. His once thriving business was in ruin.

He made me promise to check the safe deposit box weekly—he trusted no one. That September, in 1962, on the way to the bank, I ran into an old neighbor from Havana. I was embarrassed because although I knew him from childhood, I never knew his name. Why? My parents referred to him as *cara de luna*, pock marked moon face; he had a bad case of acne. He hugged me and suggested we have a quick lunch, to which I agreed, and we caught up on our families and what we knew about the other neighbors. His brother was still in Havana but he and his mom got out. If his manager hadn't come into the restaurant and greeted him, I would never have known his name was Badilla. Badilla sold shoes. He told me Americans love shoes and they purchase them for all occasions and seasons. Children's shoes were the best he said, because they grow out of them so fast. He suggested I could make a fortune selling shoes. We exchanged phone numbers and promised to keep in touch. When I returned to work, I asked the lady in personnel if I could work in the shoe department.

"No," she replied, "there are no openings!"

At dinner that night, Uncle Pepe, Aunt Carmen and I discussed my meeting with Badilla. Pepe listened carefully as I prattled on about earning more money so I could afford my own apartment and bring my parents out of Cuba. This all seemed to make sense to Pepe, and he was in agreement that I should look for a new job selling shoes. In fact, he offered to help me in that regard. He had a customer to whom he would speak the very next day. We were all pleased and excited. Then I suggested I could save extra money to go to college. That is when the laughter began.

"College in America is for millionaires," Pepe said.

Carmen suggested that getting my high school diploma would be enough for me.

Pepe ran a small watch repair booth for a jeweler. Sometimes Carmen worked with him to do the billing and keep the books. The very next day, as promised, Pepe planned to speak to his customer on my behalf. Carmen brought lunch, which she arranged on the corner of the desk, while Pepe examined a gold Rolex wristwatch. Frank, a large, prosperous man, with a good sense of humor, approached.

"Master, where is my watch?"

Pepe responded with the same sense of humor, "I'm out to lunch."

Frank's retort, "I'm out to lunch too. This is how I spend it, picking up my watch!"

Pepe winked, "Come back in twenty minutes. I'm testing it." Frank left.

Carmen said, "Be nice to him. Maybe he will give Julian a job."

Twenty minutes later, Frank returned and Pepe handed him the gold Rolex. Carmen finished typing an invoice and handed it to Pepe.

Pepe said, "Frank that is a magnificent piece. It runs perfectly now."

Frank replied, "How much do I owe you?"

Pepe handed Frank the invoice.

As Frank studied the invoice, Pepe said, "It's a fair price for a complete overhaul."

"Perhaps, but it is more than I expected to pay," Frank said.

Pepe responded, "I had to take it apart to clean it with a special machine, I replaced the mainspring, gave you an original Rolex crown, added a new crystal, detailed the case and bracelet."

"Still..." Frank said.

Pepe leaned forward and said to Frank, "I will forget what you owe me if you get my nephew a job."

Frank hesitated; then asked, "What does he do?"

"He's a seventeen-year old kid who recently arrived from Spain. Train him for anything you need."

Frank asked, "Working papers?"

Pepe was quick to respond, "I'll get you a copy."

Frank pondered the thought and added, "He'll need a suit."

Pepe said, "Done!"

Frank added, "Fix my carriage clock and you have a deal."

Frank was the district manager for a large chain of low-end shoe stores, and seemed to be deeply entrenched in Manhattan's business climate. He knew people and referred several business associates to Pepe. Frank gave Pepe an address for me to report for work within two-weeks. I was going into a six-month training program to become a store manager, and the salary was seventy-five dollars per week! I had to hand in my two week notice of resignation to the personnel department at B. Altman, and then I had to see Stanley for directions to someplace called The Bronx. I said good-bye to my co-workers and received an open invitation to party any Friday night I chose; which I did from time to time. After school I visited Stanley and asked him if he knew anyone who would buy my camera. He directed me to a large store on Thirty-Fourth Street called Willoughby's. They bought my Leica camera for sixty dollars, so I went to Macy's and bought a new pair of shoes, a few shirts and some ties. No more smocks; I had to dress up for my new job. I was excited to move on.

I called Badilla, my former neighbor from Havana, and asked him to meet me for lunch. I thanked him for suggesting the shoe business and told him about my new job. He was pleased. He told me his brother was coming to the U.S. through Mexico and his mother was thrilled. I asked him if he could help my parents get out of Cuba. He said he would see what he could do and get back to me. I was grateful.

It was October and the first day of my new job, I was eager to get to work. The air was fresh and brisk. I turned up the collar of my well-worn blue suit and found my way on the subway to The Bronx. I soon discovered the store was located in a shabby, crime ridden neighborhood. I was to report to the manager of the two-man operation. Just as I arrived, my manager, Leroy a young sharp rising star in the company chased away a wino with a baseball bat he kept by the cash register. Leroy was tall, over six feet, but slender and handsome, with an almost bubbly personality. Everything was fun to him, even chasing winos.

I'm five foot seven by contrast and wondered if fighting crime was part of the job requirements. I needed a bathroom. No bathroom. Leroy showed me a sink in the back which only ran cold water. That was where we were to urinate, wash our hands, and fill buckets of water to clean the floors and the doorway where the winos slept. The AJAX powdered cleaner helped remove the smells and stains left from the night before. There was no hot water, no toilet. My instructions were to perform any other bathroom chores at home before and after work. Where do I have lunch was answered by 'take a bus and go to East Tremont Avenue,' a commercial district with restaurants. I was stuck but I needed the job; I missed Manhattan.

Leroy instructed me how to measure the feet of a woman. "Measure the right foot first and have her stand up. Present her with the shoe as if it were a gift and invite her to try it on. That way you will avoid having to touch too many feet."

I'm a quick study, so Leroy was pleased. I was doing a good job and feeling more comfortable as customers came and went; my Spanish came in handy, and selling came easy to me, I just emulated my father. It was however, a rough day. That night, when I went home, I went from one rough neighborhood to another. As I approached my block, a kid urinated off the fire escape from the building next door to Pepe and Carmen's apartment house. At least I have a sink I mused. How long would I have to endure this life?

I applied my inventory skills to the shoe store and enjoyed having everything neatly lined up. Frank visited from time to time to check on us and seemed pleased. Leroy and I were doing a good job.

The weather was changing. I watched the winos who lived on the street, slept in doorways, and begged for money. I wondered what they did in the cold. I was cold and I didn't have a coat. Pepe gave me some old sweaters to wear under my suit jacket and I wore long underwear. I was still wearing tee shirts under my shirt and suit jacket to keep warm. One day as I stared out the window, I noticed a wino go into a thrift store across the street and come out with a coat. On my lunch hour I visited the thrift store and bought my first coat. As winter whipped through the months I bought a scarf, gloves and a hat. For the next several years, thrift shops became the main source of my apparel.

The calls from my father were infrequent and filled with despair. I felt pressured to get them out of Cuba. Back when I applied for my passport and visa in Havana, my parents applied for their passports and visas as well, as a back-up in case they too had to leave the country. While Castro seemed strong and organized, it was hoped, and some like my father believed, that the United States would not let Castro continue and everything would go back to the way it was. Once Castro declared Cuba as a communist state, and established ties with Russia, rumors of another invasion started and my parents felt they had to leave.

I remember friends and family being incredulous that the United States let Castro take over, assume power, and confiscate every foreign property in the name of the revolution. His first year in power, Castro had promised that there would be free elections within a year. Arturo and Anita assumed they would be able to follow me within a reasonable period of time, after they took care of disbursing their assets, selling the business and the buildings. But Cuba shut down; my father was unable to sell his business or his buildings. Everything existed for the revolution. About this time, I started to earn enough money to save a little every week.

· · ·

OCTOBER 23, 1962
THE CUBAN MISSILE CRISIS

Badilla called me and asked me to meet him for lunch. President Kennedy delivered a speech to the American people the night before, explaining the Cuban Missile Crisis. The week previous, an American U-2 spy plane photographed evidence of missile sites in Cuba, which was only ninety miles off the coast of Florida. As the threat of nuclear attack loomed, the United States prepared for war. Over the next few days, President John F. Kennedy and Nikita Khrushchev, General Secretary of the Communist Party of the Soviet Union, negotiated an agreement to end the crisis. Basically, the United States agreed not to invade Cuba and in return, Russia would remove their missiles from Cuba. By October twenty-eighth, the threat of nuclear war no longer existed, and the Cuban Missile Crisis was over.

Unfortunately, now that meant that Badilla could not help me get my parents out of Cuba; there was too much tension and fear in the world.

The Cold War was heating up. It started in 1947 after World War II when the temporary wartime alliance against Nazi Germany ended, and it continued for decades, basically between the Western Bloc, led by the United States and its NATO allies and the Eastern Bloc led by the Soviet Union and its allies in the Warsaw Pact.

Without direct fighting between the two superpowers, a state of political and military tension raged as proxy wars erupted in Korea and Vietnam. Significant economic and political differences defined the opposing sides; Capitalism vs. Communism. Each side armed themselves in preparation for a nuclear attack; each side was equipped with a nuclear deterrent. Both sides openly engaged in psychological warfare, espionage, competition in the space race, rivalry at sports events, and so forth. Each side sought influence in Latin America, Africa, the Middle East, and Southeast Asia. Regional conflicts around the world eventually led the super powers to seek ways to stabilize the world. But in 1962, the Cuban Missile Crisis complicated relationships between the superpowers and their allies. I was about to turn eighteen and knew I was to be called for the draft.

Leroy and I worked well together, though we had no input as to the shoes ordered for the store. Our customer base consisted mainly of urban teens who wanted high-top Converse sneakers. We were being sent black pointy shoes for the Wall Street crowd, so Leroy encouraged me to speak to Frank to request the styles that fit our customer base. What did I know; I was just a kid, according to Frank. I was ignored. However, I saw the store as an opportunity for growth, and I was learning something every day either about sales or management, and had a vested interest in seeing the store succeed.

I continued to visit retail store windows and read fashion magazines for selling ideas. My English was improving as was my knowledge of running a small business. Leroy had dreams of being in show business. He had a decent singing voice and hung out with a show business crowd on the Upper West Side where he lived. As far as the store was concerned, Leroy decided he was only interested in sales, and had no interest in the details of running the store. I pursued learning more about management and decided to do everything I could to move ahead in the company. I applied the lessons from my father regarding sales, the store window display, the inventory set up, and the review and handling of customers. Leroy taught me the company's paperwork requirements. We dressed the store window to highlight the shoes to attract our customer base, and the store continued to make money for the chain. Leroy and I were a good team and were becoming friends. Frank was happy; he left us alone; we were happy.

I checked in with Badilla from time to time, but he couldn't help me with my parents' situation, so we would have lunch, and gossip about the past.

• • •

JANUARY, 1963
MY EIGHTEENTH BIRTHDAY

I accompanied Leroy to a party in downtown Manhattan. The room was full of twenty something strangers of different ethnic and economic groups. Leroy introduced me around and announced that it was my birthday. The spirited group came together and sang a rousing rendition of the birthday song For He's A Jolly Good Fellow, and offered good wishes. I felt good and was having a great time. Nina, a beautiful wannabe actress, grabbed me and offered to give me a wonderful birthday present, which I graciously accepted through most of the night.

I staggered home, clothes askew. Carmen waited up and was furious. Pepe was curious and wanted details. I was tired and just wanted to go to bed. Carmen insisted on having a talk and began to question me.

"Where have you been all night?"

"Having fun," I answered.

Pepe seemed a bit concerned and warned, "Slow down or that thing will fall off."

I spread out on the couch and said, "I'm in love." I winked at Pepe and he half-smiled.

The next day, bleary-eyed and fatigued, I finished work while Nina waited for me. For the next several months, she and I spent a lot of time together. Finally, I had a girlfriend. We were happy together the way things were, and had no plans for the future. As a result, we didn't introduce each other to our families.

During this time, a letter arrived from the U.S. Government. It was time for me to report to the draft board. I was rejected because of my asthma and given a 4-F status. I confided my disappointment to Nina.

By November, 1963, America was in mourning. We suffered a great loss in the assassination of President John F. Kennedy. Rumors swirled that there was a connection to Fidel Castro and I feared for my family. Of course Nina knew I was Cuban.

Then in December, one day after I returned from the bank, Leroy asked me if I knew who Nina's father was. I didn't have a clue.

"You'll find out soon enough," He warned. Then he handed me a business card.

"He dropped by with a couple of goons and gave me this. He wants you in his office by noon tomorrow, so dazzle him with your charm and good manners. And watch your back." I read the name on the card; it meant nothing to me.

Later that night, I asked Pepe and Carmen if they knew who my girlfriend Nina's father was. They seemed nervous, pale actually. Pepe threw down the card and said

"He's connected."

Carmen asked, "How would Julian know that?"

I asked, "What does connected mean?"

Nina's father was well-known in New York City; his face had been in the newspapers many times. Very carefully, Pepe asked if Nina was pregnant. Of course not! I told him, we're just having fun. "Mmm," he mused, "just be there on time tomorrow."

"What should I say?" I asked.

Carmen responded quickly, "Just say that you want to marry his daughter. We're in enough trouble just being from Havana. Then she added, "We'll work it out."

Marriage, I thought? The next day, promptly at noon, I arrived at a men's clothing showroom, large and classy. A man in his forties, powerful, muscular and sharp, met me in the reception area. He looked me up and down, seemed displeased and said, "What are you wearing kid?"

I gathered he didn't like my blue suit.

Before I could respond, he shouted, "Mario! Get in here."

I stuttered as I reached out to shake his hand.

"I am Julian Vida Mr..."

Before I could get his name out and ignoring my hand, Mario a frail man in his sixties trotted to him like a puppy to a master and said, "Yes boss?"

The order was clear. "Put this suit in the garbage. Fit him with a blue suit from the new stock. When you finish, bring him into my office."

I was whisked away by Mario and led to a fitting room where I was dressed in a new suit, shirt and tie. I glanced at the price tags and was stunned. How was I going to pay for this? I was overwhelmed but continued practicing my speech in my head. I was there to ask him for his daughter's hand in marriage.

Mario led me to an opulent office and directed me to a chair opposite the boss and pleaded, "How did I do, Boss?"

The banter started. "How long have you been working for me?"

"Twenty years Boss."

"Twenty years and you're still nothing. Go back to work!"

"Thanks Boss."

As Mario turned to leave, the boss said to him, "You did okay." Then turning to me he said, "I love that guy!"

Remembering my manners, I said. "Thank you for the suit, Sir, I'll pay you every week."

"Forget it kid, it's my gift to you."

I felt the material and responded, "It is a fine suit, sir, I am grateful."

He waived his hand. He had more important things to discuss.

"Now, my daughter is crazy about you."

I added, "I love her very much, sir and..."

He cut me off again. "Cut the crap kid. I know what's going on."

As calm as I could I responded, "I am here to ask you for your daughter's hand in marriage." There, I got it out. He was not amused.

"Marriage? Tell me, how is a Cuban low life shoe salesman like you gonna take care of my princess?" There it was. I wondered if it would have been better if I were from Spain.

"My grandparents are from Spain, sir," I lamely added.

"I don't give a shit where you or your relatives are from. You're still a poor immigrant."

Although insulted, I was ready.

"I'll work very hard. I will become the manager."

He chortled, "What can you do for me?"

With great confidence, I said, "Take care of your daughter."

He stood up then, red as a beet and shouted. "The answer is NOTHING! You're nothing. There's nothing you can do for me or my daughter!"

I pleaded, "I'll do anything you want!"

He came out from his side of the desk, picked me up out of the chair by my collar and ushered me towards the door to the reception area.

"Here's what you can do for me kid. Get the fuck out of my sight!"

He pushed me into the reception area, pulled a wad of cash out of his pocket and peeled off five one hundred dollar bills. He stuffed them into my pocket. I was stunned.

"I don't want your money!"

He countered, "You think you are going to marry my daughter and get all of this?" He spread his arms.

"No!" I said. I just want to do the right thing. I don't understand."

He came towards me again, pushing me towards the front door and said, "That's right, because you're stupid. Stay away from my daughter. If I ever see you again, I bury you in that suit!"

I pushed his hand away from my back, removed the bills from my pocket, threw them on the floor and shouted, "You don't buy me!"

Surprised, he shouted for Mario. "Mario, come here and pick this up."

I walked brusquely out of the office and ran to the subway. I had no idea what I had done.

• • •

The following week, Nina showed up at the store alone. We huddled in the corner under the watchful eye of Leroy. She leaned against me and smiling cooed, "Daddy likes you."

I grabbed her arms, stared at her straight in both eyes and said bluntly, "Daddy wants to kill me."

She smiled and said, "Well, maybe he doesn't like you. But he respects you. I can tell."

"How?" I asked.

She winked, "Because he howls with laughter every time he tells the story of how Mario had to pick up the money."

I took her hand in mine. "I do love you," I said.

"You love having sex with me," She demurred.

I responded, "Yes, that too. Do you want to get married?"

Without hesitation, she replied, "No! I'm having way too much fun to worry about mopping floors and screaming kids."

A bit disappointed, I said, "Don't you love me?"

She put her arms around my neck and responded, "Yes. Just not the way you want me to." I undid her arms.

"Then maybe we shouldn't..."

Without letting me finish, she volunteered, "Don't worry, I can handle daddy."

I kissed her on the forehead and said, "But I can't." I never saw Nina again.

It was December, 1964 and school ended. I went to see Stanley at the drug store to say good-bye, because once school ended, there was no reason for me to be in that neighborhood. We really weren't friends as such, just acquaintances out of convenience. I didn't know how to have friends. I waited for him to finish work. We went out for coffee and talked about life, our dreams, and hopes for the future. He struggled economically, yet as we passed a homeless person, Stanley emptied his pockets and said to the person, "Have an easy night." That impressed me. Stanley seemed tired, a bit beaten up by life. He loved his family and wanted the best for his children, a girl about my age and a younger boy. His life was simple. Mine seemed so complicated. Overwhelmed with work and worry about my parents, disappointed by losing Nina, I wasn't thinking clearly. Against so many odds I continued to strive for success.

With great wisdom Stanley said, "Success isn't always based on what you become. Sometimes it's measured by what you overcome."

I didn't see Stanley again. He was just a nice clerk in a store, old enough to be my father. It just didn't seem appropriate to assume he could be my friend, nor did I forget his simple acts of kindness towards me. Talking with Stanley gave me a feeling of calm delight, a sense down deep that something great was to happen. I never knew his last name and continued to be amazed that this fine man would play such an extraordinary role later on in my life.

I was hoping to continue my education, and despite my aunt and uncle dissuading me, I searched for classes or programs I could afford and attend, given my work schedule. On my day off, I visited the library and read all I could about anything that interested me. It was a gift and a refuge for me. After I left the library, I would walk the streets of Manhattan and admire the beautiful architecture, the lovely display windows in the major department stores, and the people rushing everywhere. They were well-groomed, strong and determined. I loved the energy. I missed my camera.

CHAPTER EIGHT

JANUARY, 1965
SPANISH HARLEM

I still struggled to free my parents. Sometimes it seemed as if I would never see them again, but deep down inside, I knew I would. At the shoe store, my hard work and diligence paid off. By the age of twenty, I was made store manager. I took it very seriously, worked hard, and did a good job. Leroy was depending on me more and more. His show business aspirations were paying off and he was getting small roles in off off-Broadway venues. He needed to move on, so he resigned with the understanding that if he needed work, he could come back to the shoe company. It was hard to fill the position in the rough neighborhood, and he knew the business so well that he was an asset. We remained friends through many years, and I continued to party with him from time to time.

I hired an assistant. It was still a two-man operation. To protect each other, the rule was when one was outside, and if as he approached the store, he didn't see the other by the cash register inside, and there was no customer in the store, something was wrong. "Don't come in. Call the police!" The store was located in a high crime area and robberies were frequent.

Every night after closing, together we took our sales of cash, checks and credit card receipts to the night drop at the local bank. We were only allowed to leave one hundred dollars in the cash register overnight. The following day one of us would go to the bank; a teller counted the receipts from the previous night's drop, made the deposit, and gave us the receipt. Every day we had to bring back rolls of change for that day.

One day in April, my assistant went to the bank and I was alone in the store. Two men came in, looked around, and asked to see a pair of high-top sneakers.

One sat in the chair and as I bent over to measure the foot, the other one put a gun to my temple and said, "Keep your hands to your side, get up slowly, we're going to the back."

He held the gun on me and we went to the back, a long narrow space with open shelves on both sides. We walked to the middle and he told me to get on the floor. He had rope on him and tied my hands behind my back. The other perpetrator was putting shoes in a bag.

My assistant approached the store, saw the guy filling the bag, didn't see me and called the police. The other guy held me at gunpoint while his partner rummaged through the store and cleaned out the cash register. The police arrived. The guy up front tried to run from the store. My assistant swung the bag of change at him and knocked him down. A police officer came to the back, gun drawn, and through the shelves, saw the guy holding the gun against my head. The officer took a shooting stance and ordered the robber to put the gun down. He didn't. In a flash, the cop fired twice through the open shelves and hit the guy both times. The guy fell on top of my legs. I passed out for a brief time and awoke to chaos. Police, reporters, and a lot of on-lookers gathered outside the store. After all the papers were filled out, I was informed I would have to appear in court downtown to complete the process. I asked Frank if he was going to provide support, a lawyer or a company representative to accompany me.

"No," was his reply to all of it.

I was on my own and on my own time, not even money for carfare. It was a cheap company and I didn't like the way they handled the situation. With 'Manager' on my resume, it was easy to get a new job, which was a good thing because despite what happened to me and the way I was unfairly treated, Pepe and Carmen insisted I find employment immediately. Vacation/break/days off? No such thing, "Go to work!" was the mantra in my family all of my life, just go to work.

I was ready to leave the shoe business anyway. Through a pretty savvy employment agent who recognized that some of my skills were transferrable to another industry, I became a purchasing agent for a movie film processing company. The neighborhood was a great improvement, the work was interesting.

• • •

JUNE, 1965
NEW YORK CITY, NY

By June, my parents were still having difficulty finding a way out of Cuba. I called Badilla, my acquaintance from Cuba. He said he might be able to help this time but it would cost money.

That was my father's area so I contacted him and told him about *Cousin Badilla from Mexico and his greedy wife.* He understood that Badilla could get him to Mexico for a price and told me to go ahead and make the arrangements. I met with Badilla and he told me what his people needed to make it happen. There is no negotiating freedom. Later that night I told my father. He said he would take care of it; I just had to send open flight tickets for Mexico, which I did. The next day, I found Aereonaves De Mexico and purchased two one-way tickets: Havana, Cuba to Mexico City, Mexico. They were mailed special delivery. Once Anita and Arturo received the airline tickets they started the process to leave Havana. They applied to the police station for a permit, having no idea how long the process would take. I suspected my father still had money buried in the house, so I was terrified he would be caught and jailed.

Once they received their visas, three armed guards came to the house, unannounced, to take inventory. It took hours but they listed every item in our home and my father's store, which was to be turned over to the revolution. My mother cried as she told me they went through her clothing and even listed her underwear. It was cruel and humiliating. Finally, when permission was granted for them to leave the country, three armed guards returned to our home unannounced and did another inventory to confirm that nothing was missing.

My father handed the guards the keys to his home, the store and the apartment house he owned; to everything he worked for all of his life, and was given nothing in return except the opportunity for him and my mother to leave Havana with the clothes on their backs. He was fifty-two years old. They were ready to be taken to the airport under the protection of armed guards. My mother clung to a photo of me in a cardboard frame in her pocket. A guard seized it, tore the frame to make sure she wasn't hiding any contraband and gave it back to her. She kept that slit photo for years. They were taken to a hotel by the airport where they stayed for a few days. There were many people leaving as well, all housed in the tiny rooms of the hotel, with one bathroom on each floor.

• • •

I arrived home and Aunt Carmen tossed a pile of mail to me. Several letters had been backlogged. My parents were off to Mexico City to stay at the house of a couple named Sofia and Prado. They were distant relatives of friends of friends of Badilla.

Finally, Anita and Arturo arrived in Mexico. Sofia and Prado were fat and happy farmers and fruit importers who lived on the outskirts of Mexico City. Their cluttered house rocked with frenetic activity. Children and farm animals flittered freely. My mother cleaned and my father helped feed and clean the animals. My mother had a visa problem and needed additional time in Mexico City. This did not sit well with Prado. He figured that they would be with him twelve weeks longer than originally planned. According to him, twelve weeks equaled eighty-four days, and with three meals a day that equaled two hundred fifty-two meals for two people and that came to about five hundred meals Sofia had to prepare.

My father offered to pay for the meals; my mother offered to cook them.

"Cook?" said Prado. "No, let's not spoil my wife."

"I'll help you in your business," my father volunteered.

"What do you know about the fruit business?" Prado inquired.

"What do you want?" my father asked.

Prado looked my father up and down and said. "You haven't changed that shirt since you've been here. Obviously it is your favorite. Give it to me."

"I'll have Julian send more money," my father assured him. Prado took a pistol from his pocket, waived it at my father and said.

"The shirt will do. Or would you like to visit Fidel's Punishment Pavilion on Isla de Pĩnos?"

My father reluctantly removed his shirt and turned it over to Prado. No doubt Prado enjoyed the American fifty dollar bills sewn into the cuffs and one peso gold coins behind the buttons.

When my parents told me the story, my mother quipped, "It was a good thing he didn't ask me for my blouse. I had gold chains sewn into my collar, American one-hundred dollar bills in the cuffs, and two peso coins behind my buttons, so he didn't get away with too much. Frankly they would have paid him more. My parents did not have an easy time.

• • •

OCTOBER, 1965
SPANISH HARLEM, NEW YORK

Unfortunately, within six months, the film processing movie company was purchased by another company that was relocated out of state and I was out of a job. My parents were due to arrive around Thanksgiving. Pepe was working with Frank to get them jobs, yet I was still angry with Frank for the way he treated me after the robbery, so I refused to ask for any favors. I had been searching for an apartment for us. Everything seemed to fall apart for me, but everything was in place for my parents.

Uncle Pepe called upon Frank who arrived at my uncle's place of work, and where Pepe thanked him for coming.

"Are you sure I am not interrupting your lunch, Master?" Frank asked sarcastically.

Pepe responded, "You never interrupt, my friend."

Then he handed Frank a Rolex watch. "Take a look at this Rolex Prince Platinum, mint."

Frank asked, "How much?"

Pepe responded, three thousand five hundred." Frank put the watch down.

"Too much for me," He started to leave. Pepe said, "You can have it for two thousand five hundred, and another favor." Frank was intrigued.

"Who is it this time?"

"My brother and sister-in-law."

"What does he do?"

"He had his own antique store in Havana. He also designs, constructs and installs chandeliers."

"Perfect. The wife?"

Pepe answered, "She'll clean up."

Got any more relatives coming over?" Frank inquired.

"I hope not." Pepe answered.

I called Badilla and we had lunch. I told him my predicament. He reassured me that people will always need shoes and told me about a store in upper Manhattan. I had to go back to what I knew best, back to selling shoes.

By the end of October, my new job was going well. The store was located in upper Manhattan on a busy commercial street next door to a coffee shop. The pay was higher, the customers more demanding, but they paid more for high quality designer shoes. As a result, I earned more money as a salesman on commission than I had as a manager; no more management for me—it was a thankless job. But I had to meet a quota and if I failed to meet the figures set for me, I would be let go. I was being watched carefully. One day the district manager appeared and joined in the review of my work. There must have been a full-moon the night before because every nightmare customer one could think of appeared. I had to be at my best; I took the challenge.

Besides people forgetting their wallets, losing their credit cards, changing their minds several times, and basically wasting my time, an elderly lady was escorted, or should I say dragged in by two nurses, one on either side. Her feet barely touched the floor. The trio approached me and the elderly lady said in a very weak voice, "Young man, do have shoes for me?"

"Madame," I said, "We have shoes that will last you a lifetime."

I heard my co-workers giggling behind me. I led her to a chair, measured her foot and sold her three pairs of shoes after showing her and helping her try on at least twenty pairs.

My next customer, a young man, tried on a pair of shoes and walked backwards right out of the store into the street. I followed him out, led him back in; he merely said, "It's the only way I know for sure that they fit."

"Good," I said. "Wear them home. Cash or charge?"

An old man barged in and slammed three shoe boxes on the counter and barked, "I want my money back!"

I inspected the first box of women's shoes and remarked, "These shoes were sold three years ago, you see?" I turned the shoe over and on the shank (on the sole by the heel) in crayon the sales person wrote the month and year it was sold.

The man was unmoved, "She's dead! Never wore them."

I inspected the other two boxes and found the same; women's shoes, one pair unworn and the other pair lightly used.

"The best I can do is offer store credit."

"Unacceptable," he bellowed.

"A store credit has no expiration date," I assured him. The old man scanned the shelves, focused on the men's shoes and simply declared, "That's acceptable!"

I issued a store credit and suggested he return the following week during our next sale. He knowingly winked, thanked me and bolted from the store.

Jerome, my manager came over and complimented me. I thought I was through for the day when a gum chewing forty something year old woman with a bird face and spindly legs came in and demanded service. Jerome nodded for me to help her. I followed her to the sale rack and she yelled at me.

"Hey you, all these shoes on sale?"

I replied, "Only those marked."

She grabbed a pair off the rack and ordered me to ring her up. I did and handed her the slip.

Perturbed, she boomed, "You said they were marked down."

"No, I said only those marked."

"What? I don't understand your accent. Where are you from?"

Having nothing to hide, I said "Cuba." I was not prepared for her response.

"Huh, look at this fancy Spic. I bet you are a communist plant. You lied to me!"

Jerome heard her; all the customers and workers in the store heard her. I was incredulous.

"I'll have my manager take care of you." I responded and turned my back on her.

"How dare you turn your back on me!" she screamed.

Before I could respond Jerome stepped between us.

To Jerome, she said, "You ought to hire people who can speak English."

Jerome stated, "He was clear with you."

She retorted, "You gonna mouth off to me too, boy?"

I guess she touched another nerve. Jerome voided the sale, then took her by the arm, led her to the door and opened it wide.

In a raised voice he said, "Take your business elsewhere."

She huffed, "Well, I never..."

He then placed his arm around me and said, "You gotta learn to act, not react."

His advice was sound. But from that day on, I never revealed my background as Cuban; to acquaintances, customers or the people with whom I worked, As far as anyone knew, I lived in Spain before coming to America.

I went home that night spent, and decided to just rest. Aunt Carmen and Uncle Pepe wanted to have a talk. It always involved a complaint; a request for a favor, or more commonly, more money. Long ago, I stopped telling them my salary and just paid whatever weekly rent they wanted.

"We found an apartment for you in the building, you can move in right away." Uncle Pepe said.

The truth was I couldn't wait to get out of there. I had been looking for an apartment for my parents out of the building. On my days off I was even searching in Queens and Brooklyn. I thought Carmen and Pepe would feel abandoned. Perhaps I was wrong.

Aunt Carmen said, "Well you can't all stay here!"

Of course she was right and I was grateful that they did the legwork. Maybe it would be good to have my parents close to family as they made their transition. Yes, I was happy and eager to move down three floors.

· · ·

On my way to work I accidentally bumped into the prettiest blond I had seen in ages. During lunch I spotted her again; I was smitten. Later that afternoon, I signed the lease for the new apartment, moved out of my aunt and uncle's apartment, and started fixing up the place for my parents as best I could. I had three weeks to get everything ready for their arrival. I bought furniture on credit and added touches from the thrift stores. I bought my parents coats for the winter months, and felt free for a while living alone.

With Frank's business card in hand, Aunt Carmen visited Blue Brothers Lighting Emporium in mid-Manhattan and met with Seymour the manager. It was a mix of showroom and factory. The company was known for their grand chandeliers. My father was a master craftsman who designed and constructed chandeliers before Castro took over, and was written about in a lighting magazine as one of the best craftsman in the Caribbean. Seymour was impressed. As I matured, I too was impressed.

"Does he do installations?" Seymour asked.

"He does it all, design, construction and installation," she then added, "and the wife will clean up. All I need from you is a letter of employment for each."

Seymour added, "And all I need is a letter of sponsorship for each and a guarantee they will show up." Everything was in place. I was eager to see my parents, and began rethinking my position at work; I thought maybe management would be more stable. I had to take care of them.

It was Friday. The shoe store was quiet, and as I looked out the window I saw the blond next door. She was gorgeous.

"Her name is Monique, she's the new waitress," Jerome said.

"I'm in love."

"Don't bother," he replied, "everyone around here has already tried."

"I can look, can't I?" I started to fix the displays.

Jerome said, "Aren't you going out tonight?"

"No more partying," I answered, "I want you to consider me for a manager's position. I need a career, not a job."

"You've been doing good work so I'll consider it, but the company gives preference to married men with families."

My eyes drifted towards the window as Monique passed by. "I'll marry someday."

BOOK IV

New York City, Reunited

CHAPTER NINE

THANKSGIVING DAY, 1965
JULIAN'S APARTMENT

The apartment was clean. I placed doilies on every surface and dotted each room with religious figurines, and I hung a crucifix over the bed. Spanish food products lined the kitchen counter. I left Spanish newspapers and magazines in the living room, and opened all the window shades to let in as much light as I could. I tried to make it as close as possible to what my parents knew, so they would be comfortable, though I didn't have the funds for the expensive furniture and antiques I had growing up.

Then it was off to JFK Airport in New York City to pick them up. I carried their coats, and in my father's coat pockets placed his precious three knotted handkerchiefs, his bank statement and a cigar. The airport was quiet. There they were, dressed for warm weather carrying shopping bags tied with ropes. I ran to them. My mother in a heap of anxiety collapsed in my arms and wept. I held her for a long time. As passengers disembarked, they seemed to glare at her. She swooned. My father was stoic. I hadn't seen them for four and a half years.

"Why is everyone staring at her?" I asked.

"Ignore her," he said, "she had a little fit."

I had no idea what he was talking about. I placed a coat around my mother and attempted to hug my father. He was like concrete. I handed him his coat and the cigar. I was excited and babbled, "Welcome to New York. There is so much I want to show you."

My mother said quietly, "I've had enough sightseeing. Take me home."

My father slipped on the coat and said, "You have something for me?"

"Check the pockets, I grinned."

He inspected each package closely. He checked the key to the safe deposit box, and took several minutes to review the bank statement.

"I notice one of the packages has been tampered with," he said.

"It happened on the third pick-up, I'll explain later but it's all there, Papa. No one took anything."

He was skeptical and just stared at me with dead cold eyes. I never understood why he didn't trust me; I did everything he asked. While he continued to massage the handkerchiefs and review the statement, I was left holding all the bags.

I hailed a taxi. Arturo leaned back and chewed on the unlit cigar while Anita seemed faint. I sat up front with the driver. The Spanish driver started the engine and immediately Anita banged on the window, "Open the window!"

"What's the problem?" the driver inquired.

"I'll suffocate and die." Right then I knew what happened on the plane.

"Leave the window open," I said.

The driver responded, "Give me a break buddy, it's winter!" He stopped the taxi, "Get out! There are plenty of other fares."

I responded, "Five dollars over the meter plus a tip."

The window remained opened. I thought I saw my father smile. I had learned how to negotiate and get things done.

We arrived at the apartment. I showed them the lobby and the mailboxes. Immediately, Arturo ripped our name off the mailbox.

"How are we going to get our mail?" I asked.

Arturo quipped, "Post office box. Never let anyone know where you live." Then to Anita he asked, "Do you think we were followed?"

"By whom," I asked, "you're free here, you are safe."

I was worried. I showed them the laundry room; Arturo took note of the coins needed to operate the washer and dryer. I showed them the garbage disposal!

We proceeded to the apartment. Arturo and Anita were unhappy.

"Too small, too dark, because there are not enough lamps, no chandeliers, junky furniture," they complained incessantly. The first thing they did was to go through the apartment and close the shades. No window light allowed; people might be watching. Anita removed a statue of the Virgin Mary from one of her bags that was tied with ropes and placed it on the dresser. Next, she placed a statue of Jesus on the T.V., St. Lazarus made it atop the refrigerator.

My father laid out the three packages, untied each handkerchief and counted and reviewed every coin and piece of jewelry. Then they put on all the jewelry they could fit on their wrists and around their necks, and pranced around the apartment. I just stood aside and watched the show. Years of communism left its mark. They wore the jewelry for the rest of the day and evening.

Arturo asked, "Pepe's apartment, is it bigger?"

"No," I replied.

"Good," was his response.

Anita admired her jewelry, "Carmen's going to be so jealous."

Arturo rechecked the bank statement against shreds of paper he brought with him. Pepe and Carmen were coming for dinner. I was cooking, but first I went for a walk.

Carmen and Pepe arrived, arms filled with clothing, linens and kitchenware. Dangling from Pepe's pinkie was a box of pastries. I placed the pastries on a plate and for some reason, cut the store label off the box and placed it in my wallet.

We put the gifts away. I had everyone sit around the table while I served. There was a lot of excitement and chatter—it was a happy time. I had my family together, safe and, well safe! I stood by as the playful banter exploded. It quickly changed to competition.

"I bought you the best pastries in the city," Pepe said.

"They'll never be as good as the ones I bought in Havana."

"It's good to see you haven't changed," said Pepe.

"You got fat," replied Arturo.

Pepe responded with, "You got old."

Carmen interceded, "There's so much to talk about."

Arturo began, "Money, I gave you five hundred dollars when you left Havana."

Carmen answered, "You couldn't possibly think we owe you anything?"

"You didn't use it to come home, so what did you do with it?" asked Arturo.

The conversation was getting heated so I interjected, "You could thank them for all they've done all these years and for the gifts they just brought."

Anita answered, "Why? They're family."

I needed to change the subject and tried talking about my job. Arturo was having none of it.

He pointed at me, "You! What happened to all the money I sent you for deposit?"

Shocked, I responded immediately, "I deposited it. You have the statement. Whatever I received I deposited, as you instructed."

Arturo didn't believe me. "By my calculations, some money is missing. So you steal from me too?"

Both Carmen and Pepe came to my defense and explained that whatever came, in whatever form, I always took it directly to the bank and deposited it. I never took a dime of my father's money. It was all for them. Everything I had I earned.

Arturo lamented, "How can I believe any of you?"

"Then don't!" Pepe answered.

Arturo continued, practically in tears. "I lost everything, everything I worked for all of my life, do you have any idea what that feels like?"

We were all silent. Carmen whispered, "No."

Dinner was short. Arturo extended his right arm directly in front of him and moved it across the table as if to bless it.

After a short time, he announced, "Dinner is over." Anita, Carmen and Pepe put down their flatware.

"I'm still hungry!" I said.

Anita offered, "Your father is finished."

Arturo banged his fist on the table, "Dinner is over! I am the king of this family and I am not stepping down."

• • •

Our living arrangement was the same as I had with Uncle Pepe and Aunt Carmen. Arturo and Anita slept in the bedroom; I slept on the couch behind a sheet hung from the ceiling. I didn't sleep well that night. I was torn between gratitude that my parents were safe and with me after having been separated for so many years, and guilt because I was upset by their behavior and longed for my own living space. They had a few days before they started work so I thought maybe over the weekend they would settle in and we would re-connect in a happier way.

Then the BANGING started. First it seemed it was on the walls, then the ceiling. It was seven a.m., the day after Thanksgiving. I ran to the bedroom. There was my father with nails in his teeth, banging nails into the walls in the bathroom and near his bed. The banging on the ceiling was from neighbors who had been awakened and disturbed by the noise.

"Papa, please stop the banging," I pleaded.

"Not until I'm finished hanging my underwear to dry," he replied.

He put a clothesline in the bathroom.

"You can use the dryer in the laundry room," I told him.

"No! I just saved a quarter."

"Don't you hear the neighbors banging on the ceiling?" I cried.

His response, "They can bang and I can't?"

Were they always like this, I thought. It was going to be a tough day. I dressed and went for a walk.

I arranged for a few days off and wanted my parents to get acclimated to the building, the neighborhood, etc. I wanted to show them the Manhattan I had learned to love. They had no interest, so I led them through the neighborhood to the local stores and gently suggested they learn English. They saw no need given the neighborhood we were in. That saddened me.

I decided to go to the library for a couple of hours and informed Arturo and Anita that I would be gone for a short time.

"No library, take your mother food shopping. You know she's no good with money."

Off mama and I went to the supermarket. As soon as we entered, she scanned the shelves and ran out of the store crying. I went after her outside and consoled her, totally unaware of what she had lived through.

Why are you so upset?" I asked.

"The government lied to us and said there was little food and blamed the United States embargo for the rationing, but it was too dangerous to speak up against The Revolution. About a year after you left, every family was given the *Libreta de Abastecimiento.*"

As she explained, it was a supplies booklet for food and household rations. Most of the products were sold in the *bodegas,* convenience stores specializing in distribution of the rations. The government established the rations for each person, and the number of times they were allowed to purchase them.

Meat, poultry or fish were sold at the local *carniceria* or meat store. Other products like light bulbs and cigarettes were included in these booklets. Milk was distributed according to age; children under seven and people over sixty-five; pregnant women and the ill were given a litre of milk per day. My parents were healthy but those with medical problems requiring special diets had to have a doctor's letter indicating the products needed. There was significant black market activity regarding food distribution, and harsh penalties were meted out in the form of extended jail terms if one was caught. One would spend more time in jail if they killed a cow rather than a human.

Anita expected a small store with few products on the shelves. She was simply overwhelmed by the size of the store and the amount of products available in every category. I had no idea what that must have been like back in Havana. As long as I had money to buy what I wanted, I could choose among the vast array of products. In Cuba those choices were gone. Before we went back into the store, she insisted we call Arturo to join us. We waited for him to arrive and the three of us went back into the store; for them it was like a museum. We spent most of the afternoon looking at fresh, frozen and packaged food. They were stunned by the choices of cheeses, breads, meats, fish, fruit and vegetables. We indulged.

I promised that every Sunday would be food shopping day for the three of us. The following Sunday morning we were all well-groomed and dressed in our best, ready for what I thought was a day out together as a family. Before we left, my parents followed the well-worn ritual of their own. My father, in a brown suit and hat methodically unplugged table lamps and wall lamps. My mother, coiffed, overly made-up, and dressed in a tight skirt, low-cut blouse and spiked heels followed behind and closed and locked every window in each room.

I stood by the door and waited! It was eerily familiar.

Anita attempted to get Arturo's attention, "I must have spent two hours curling my hair for you. Do you like it?"

Indifferently, he ordered, "Don't interrupt me. Get the pillowcase."

The pillowcase contained a Wonder Bread Wrapper. She removed the Wonder Bread Wrapper and waited while Arturo unplugged the telephone and handed it to her. She carefully wrapped the telephone in the pillow case and stored it in the Wonder Bread Wrapper, which my father closely inspected. They proceeded to the kitchen, where Arturo placed the new telephone I bought them in the refrigerator.

"Good, they break in, they can't up my telephone bill." He continued to unplug small appliances and straighten the gas jets.

As my father locked the door, he announced, "I want dinner on the table by six on the dot."

Food shopping with them became a joyful experience. Arturo took charge; he inspected everything that went into the cart and either gave his approval or it went back on the shelf. He monitored the cashier carefully and before we left the store, checked and double checked the receipt against the items in the cart. I proudly stood aside as they reminded me of how things used to be.

Anita cooked constantly. Then came the mystery of Carmen's pots. The two families shared many meals and every time we ate in Carmen and Pepe's apartment, Anita would look at Carmen's pot rack on the wall and marvel at how shiny her pots were. Frequently at night, Anita would be in our kitchen scrubbing her pots. She never could quite get the shine that Carmen had. It drove her crazy. She called me at work more than once and begged me to find out Carmen's secret.

That Monday, while I was at work, there was a knock on the door to the apartment. Anita and Arturo huddled by the door whispering, "Who could it be?"

"Mailman," came the response! Arturo and Anita refused to open the door.

"I hear you, I need a signature."

They continued to refuse to open the door, so the mailman gave up and left a notice on the door. When I returned from work, they gave me the notice. I was angry.

"Why didn't you accept the letter?"

"How do we know he is really a mailman?" they reasoned.

I had to get up an hour earlier to get to the post office to pick up the letter.

I brought it home for them and said, "See, this is for you. It contains your employment letters from your new boss."

Anita waived her hand and said, "Okay, now we have it. Did you find out how Carmen gets her pots so shiny?"

We all have our priorities.

I took Arturo and Anita to work their first day. I tried to explain that Seymour would be their boss. But that did not sit well with Arturo. Seymour was nice and spoke some Spanish. My father spoke broken English, which he had picked up from American tourists over the years prior to Castro, much of which he had forgotten. My mother could only say, 'Beeutiful!' Everything was 'beeutiful'. I prayed they would not get fired. Seymour explained their hours were seven a.m. to three-thirty p.m. with a half hour lunch and two fifteen minute breaks. My father insisted on lunch at noon. That was fine with Seymour, who gave us a tour and thanked me for interpreting. He led them to what was to become Arturo's work bench piled high with crystals, chandelier parts and tools. Arturo was in his element. He just had one question.

My father said incredulously to Seymour, "Me report to you?"

"Yes, directly to me," Seymour responded.

Pointing to Anita, Arturo announced, "Okay, she report to me. You tell me what you want she do. I see to it."

That didn't feel good to me, but Seymour was okay with it, and handed Arturo a broom. Arturo handed it to Anita and told her where to start.

Seymour shook my hand, winked and said, "They'll be fine."

I wondered what *his* father was like.

I went to work somewhat calm. There was Monique, taking a cigarette break. She was like a light in the storm. Magnificent Monique, all I could do was look from afar. I thought I saw a shadow of a smile from her.

CHAPTER TEN

JANUARY, 1966
FAMILY TOGETHER

It was my twenty-first birthday; it had been almost eight years since my family was all together in Cuba. Again, Pepe brought pastries from a bakery across town. I made a note to visit it someday. I invited Badilla and his mother and brother to join us, and it was a gala time. There was lots of chatter as they traveled down memory lane together. We all missed Havana. Prior to Castro's takeover, Cuba, the largest island in the Caribbean, was a haven for tourists and investors, and considered relatively well advanced by Latin American standards. The consensus was it would never be returned to its former glory.

In February, I applied to Hunter College's adult education classes and took Conversational English and some business classes. Arturo and Anita thought it was a waste of time, and had no trouble reminding me of that every night when I returned from school. Why, because I threw off their schedule. Dinner by six p.m., sleep by nine p.m. Many nights I arrived home after ten. They were confused. One of those nights, when it was after ten, Arturo and Anita waited by the door.

"We want you home by nine p.m.," they demanded.

"My classes end late. What is the problem?" I asked.

"We worry about you," My mother said.

I was livid and lost my temper.

"You didn't worry about me when you sent me out of Cuba with a suit which could have gotten me killed, to people I didn't know, in a foreign country with no support! You didn't worry when you sent me to New York, the docks in New Jersey at five in the morning, to some basement in Chinatown, or the lunatic on Park Avenue. I could have been killed getting what was yours. I was just a naïve kid. How could you do that to me?"

I searched my father's eyes; his dead, cold eyes.

"Humph. It was just business," he nonchalantly replied.

I didn't talk to them for a few days.

A couple of days later I was at work staring out of the window at Monique. I was making headway with her, slowly but surely with friendly waves, nods and broad smiles. One morning she actually wished me a good day. I returned the wish. Later in the afternoon I was happily waiting on a customer when I looked up and through the display window I saw my mother's hands and face pressed against the glass.

My father, cigar in hand, placed his chin on her shoulder and leaned in. I left my customer with a shoe dangling from her foot and ran outside. I pulled my parents away from the window.

"What are you doing here?" I demanded.

"Watching you work," Arturo answered.

"Why?" I was incredulous.

Anita chimed in, "So we know you are okay."

And there was Monique on her cigarette break. She smiled at me. I was embarrassed. I moved my parents out of earshot of Monique and said to them, "Please go home, please."

Anita said, "Since we finish early, we decided we will pick you up every day."

"Do you really think I need you to help me find my way home?" I inquired.

Arturo answered, "What else do you have to do? You work, you go home. Eat dinner at six, go to sleep at nine, that's life!"

"That's your life!" I retorted, "Please go home. I will see you later."

They left. Monique was still outside on her break. I sincerely hoped she did not understand Spanish.

"Your parents are cute," she said.

"So are you, I replied." We both went back to work.

A couple of days later, just before noon, I was staring out of the window at Monique when Jerome came rushing over. "Julian, your father's boss is on the phone. There's an emergency."

I grabbed the phone, took down the necessary information as Jerome stood by. "I have to get to the hospital."

"Go ahead, take care."

I dashed out of the store and bumped into Monique as I hailed a cab.

"I'm so sorry, emergency, are you okay?"

"Yes, yes," she assured me. "Go, I hope all is okay."

With her blessing, I jumped in a cab, gave the driver the name of the hospital and turned around to wave at Monique. She waived back.

I watched while an emergency doctor examined my mother. My father was nowhere to be seen.

"I'll order some tests, but I think she'll be just fine. Wait outside and I will have the nurse prepare her."

I went to the waiting room. While I paced back and forth, Arturo arrived, cup of coffee in hand.

"Where have you been?" I asked.

"Twelve o'clock, I eat lunch," with his napkin he wiped his chin, "meatloaf pretty good. So how long is this going to take?"

After a while, the doctor came out.

"She's fine. You can take her home."

Arturo whispered in my ear; then I approached the doctor. "My father asks that you admit her to the hospital. She thinks she is dying."

The doctor said gently, "I cannot justify an admission for constipation. A mild laxative and a change in diet would help."

On the way home, I stopped to buy a laxative. I was exhausted. It made Arturo and Anita happy that I went to sleep by nine. The next morning, my father stood guard at the bathroom door.

"How is she?" I asked.

"It's not going to be a good day," he said.

"Didn't she take the laxative?" I asked.

"American doctors, what do they know?"

I stopped at the flower shop and bought a bouquet of flowers for Monique. It caused quite a stir when I entered the restaurant and gave them to her. The wait-staff were all a-twitter. Monique was impressed and pleased.

"Good morning, I assume all is well?" she said.

"No. But I want you to have these although they are not as beautiful as you." I heard a collective, "Ahh!" That night I had school so I arrived home after nine.

"You're late!" Anita scorned.

"You know I had school."

"A waste of time," my father added.

"Why didn't you call?" Anita chimed in.

"A *third* time?" I said sarcastically.

Anita was miffed, "Well, we have to know where you are."

I stood between them and placed my arms around each of them. "Are the jobs going well?" I asked.

"Why?" Arturo boomed.

"I want to make sure you are happy and can handle the rent," I said.

Another boom, "Why?"

"I need my own place," I announced.

"Why?" the broken record asked.

"Because maybe I want to have a girl over once in a while."

Without a beat, Arturo spoke with great authority, "You don't know the difference between a hair itch and a hard-on. What do you know about girls?"

With pride and a bit of bravado, I responded, "I've had more sex in the past couple of years than you probably had your whole lifetime."

Arturo did not like that. "You talk shit! If you want privacy to work out your sexual appetite, we'll hang another sheet!"

Anita said, "Don't I cook enough?"

I hugged my mother and said, "You are a wonderful cook."

Nine o'clock they were in bed; the door to the bedroom closed. I settled in on the couch and stayed up late to read. From behind the door a voice rumbled, "Go to sleep, it's after nine o'clock." My decision was made.

On my days off, I looked for an apartment. I arrived home from school one night and Anita and Arturo met me at the door.

Anita cooed, "Ooh my baby's home."

"Stop it, I'm not a baby." I was still cross with them.

"Don't talk to your mother like that," Arturo said.

Exasperated, I said, "Fine! The baby is leaving. I took a studio apartment. That means one room."

Anita quipped, "In the building? Give me a key."

"No, a borough away, in Queens."

"So," the king stated, "you abandon your family again?"

"You're the one who sent me away, remember?" I answered.

His reply, "That was business."

Monique and I were developing a relationship. We saw each other every day, stole quick hugs and soft kisses, had lunch together and spent endless hours on the phone in the evenings after eight when her child went to sleep. She was a twenty-one year old single mom; I was a twenty-one year old guy eager to have a real date, and when I told her that, she simply said, I am not interested in dating, I'm looking for a husband and father for my child."

I appreciated her candor and wondered if I was up to the job. Jerome noticed my budding relationship with Monique, slapped me on the back and said, "You are the man!"

"How about that management position?" I inquired.

I loved my apartment; it was perfect, quiet, and neat. It was located in Queens not far from where Monique lived. I took a short lease. I earned enough money to buy the basics and made myself quite comfortable, all the while building up my savings account. From the day I moved in, promptly at nine o'clock at night the phone rang. It was my mother wishing me a good sleep and inquiring about my day. This happened every night of my life. If I was out, the rule was I had to call her promptly at nine to say goodnight. Over the years it took some maneuvering and more than once it created friction with whomever I was with. I soon learned it was easier to get the call out of the way than risk the panic of Anita and Arturo when, if they couldn't reach me you see, they weren't averse to sending the police to find me, claiming something happened to me, otherwise I would have called. Calling was as much a part of my routine as brushing my teeth.

· · ·

JANUARY, 1967
TWENTY-SECOND BIRTHDAY

Remembering that pastry shop label from the pastries Uncle Pepe bought when my parents arrived, I went to the East side of Manhattan where it was located and bought myself a birthday cake and my favorite pastries.

I was having my first party in my own apartment, and it felt wonderful. Besides my parents, Aunt Carmen and Uncle Pepe, I invited Monique and her daughter. I was nervous. My family arrived first; Aunt Carmen helped me arrange the pastries on a dish and made the coffee. My parents watched TV. When the doorbell rang, I jumped. Aunt Carmen and Uncle Pepe welcomed Monique and her daughter Dannielle just as they welcomed Irene so many years before. My mother? Well she was again jealous.

Monique was lovely and appropriately mannered. I took their coats, and Monique introduced her adorable four-year old to everyone; little Dannielle was well behaved It was the first time I was meeting the child, and had prepared a corner for her to play in, and said something like, "Mommy is so proud of you and she told me you like dolls."

Her eyes lit up and she shook her head yes. I removed a wrapped present from the closet and gave it to her. It was a big doll and she was happy to play in the corner. Monique joined the ladies and everyone seemed to be getting along fine. Aunt Carmen led the conversation and translated for Anita. At one point Monique put her arm through mine and announced,

"Julian wants to take care of me and Dannielle. I'm going to let him." My parents were silent. Maybe they didn't understand.

Pepe spoke up and repeated, "*Let* him?"

"Absolutely," Monique added, "I'm sure he'll learn to love Dannielle, I'm going to go for it!"

"Go for it?"

I wondered why he was repeating everything she said. I was blinded by her beauty and frankly didn't hear the subtext like Pepe did. At one point, little Dannielle dropped a cup of water. Monique went over to help her as did Carmen and Anita.

Anita said out loud, "Estupida!" and slapped Dannielle's little hands. Danielle cried.

Arturo mocked her, "Boo hoo."

Monique confronted Anita, "Why did you hit my child?"

I stepped between them and said something like, "My mother is nervous around children and was afraid she would hurt herself."

I picked up Danielle and played with her in the corner with the doll. Giggles and laughter soon replaced the tears and anger. She soon forgot about the spilt water, but I was remembering all the beatings at the hands of my own mother. Yes, I would take care of Monique and Dannielle. It would be just the three of us; happy and content. Conversation halted among the adults. All eyes were on me and Dannielle. It was time for Monique and

Dannielle to go home. We said our good-byes and they left; my family remained.

Pepe asked with some concern, "Do you realize what you are getting yourself into?"

"If you're asking if I love her, the answer is yes," I answered.

Anita and Arturo did not take me seriously, dismissed the notion that I was getting married, and scoffed at the thought of me being a father. To them I was still a child and as far as they were concerned they weren't going to waste another moment talking about it. They had more important things to discuss. Pots! Anita insisted that Carmen tell her how she kept the pots on her pot rack so shiny.

"Easy," said Carmen, "they've never been used—they are strictly for show."

I howled. If Carmen only knew how many nights Anita stood over that sink scrubbing and scraping. Anita was not amused. I needed the laugh.

CHAPTER ELEVEN

JUNE, 1968
CITY HALL

Monique and I were married in the morning at City Hall. We went out for lunch, took the subway uptown, and by afternoon we were both at work. It was fun, we were happy. We went to work together, went home together, and saw each other all day. Dannielle was in school and then taken care of by Monique's mother. Jerome gave me the management position, and I felt secure within the growing company. Monique had a substantial following of customers who tipped well so we were doing okay. I hoped we could save enough to buy a small house and live happily ever after.

Shortly after my twenty-fourth birthday, I was locking up the store while Monique stood by; she looked ill.

"Are you okay?" I asked out of concern.

"Just tired," she said. Then she removed a flyer from her bag and showed it to me. It was an advertisement for a new restaurant downtown.

"What about it?" I asked.

"They offered me a job," she said with some hesitation.

"You mean you applied for a job and they hired you?" I asked.

"Yes," was all she said. I was angry.

"Without telling me, why?" It bubbled out.

"I'm not like your parents. I need to breathe without you smelling me all day."

"What do you really want?" I asked.

"Another child," she said.

"No kids. I told you that before we married. It was to be just the three of us."

"I thought you would change your mind," she lamented.

My response, "We're struggling just to get by! Another kid will tie me up in the pocket."

• • •

It was Monique's day off. I expected dinner on the table, but when I arrived home, I noticed Monique was casually dressed; no lipstick, no shoes. There was Eddie, her first husband; twenty-seven year old Eddie, handsome, athletic, street smart and dressed in casual slacks and a tee-shirt.

"Hi honey, we have company, meet my ex, Eddie," Monique sing-songed as I shook his hand.

"If you're staying for dinner, put your shirt on." I demanded. Eddie was apologetic.

"Sorry man, I was playing on the floor with Danielle and I got hot." Eddie put his shirt on. I kissed Dannielle on the forehead before I excused myself and went to our bedroom to wash up for dinner. My stomach was in knots. I heard dishes crash. I ran to the kitchen.

"Are you okay?" Monique was flushed; she wiped a smile off her face. Eddie held back a giggle. They were like two kids who had a secret.

"I'm fine, I tripped." Monique lamely said, her eyes rolling back and forth to Eddie.

Dannielle piped up, "Daddy bought me a new doll and put me in for my nap today." I looked directly at Eddie and challenged him.

"So, you've been here all day?" Then I looked at Monique and stated, "You two look very comfortable with each other. Anything you want to tell me?"

Monique exhaled, breathed deeply and said. "Eddie and me, we're getting back together."
Eddie added, "For Dannielle's sake." I was incredulous.

"For Dannielle's sake," Monique continued, "you don't want any kids and she's lonely."

I shot back. "We'll buy her a puppy." Monique lit a cigarette. She needed courage.

"The truth is, we made a mistake," Eddie added, "we thought you'd be okay with this, you know."

I answered, *"We*? How long?"

Eddie moved to Monique's side; he claimed his territory. "Right after you got married. I love her man."

"Obviously she doesn't love me." I had no idea where my stomach was, but I felt my heart shatter.

Monique asked, "You're not mad are you? I really care about you."

I was stunned, "You care about me? I love you with all that I am. How could you do this to me?"

Eddie said shamelessly, "Listen, we don't want any trouble."

I glared at them both. "Trouble? No trouble. All she really needs is a wallet and a cock. She's all yours."

I packed what I could and with two suitcases stood in front of my parents' apartment and looked up at the window. I hoisted my belongings and entered the building. I crawled onto the couch and turned on the light to read. From the bedroom, I heard.

"Shut the light".

I responded, "Go to sleep!"

Arturo barreled into the room and stated, "My house, my rules. Lights out!"

I slammed the book shut and turned off the light. Arturo claimed his territory.

Within a short time, by mutual consent, the marriage was annulled. The papers arrived at work. Jerome delivered them to me, watched as I opened the documents, signed them, and returned them to the messenger.

"Sorry it didn't work out, man," he was sympathetic.

"This whole situation cost me plenty," I complained.

CHAPTER TWELVE

JUNE, 1970
NEW YORK CITY, NY

Now that I was twenty-five, I was feeling old, broken and a bit lost. I had to start over economically and start saving again so I could afford my own place. Living with my parents was a challenge. They charged me twenty-five dollars a week for the couch and an occasional dinner. I couldn't work more than six days a week in the shoe store, so I thought of ways to earn extra money. I found a stamp club, and sold more of my stamp collection. The man who bought them had a wonderful collection of stamps from Israel, which made me think of Benjamin, Ruth and Irene and the bakery in Havana. Then I thought about Stanley and his acts of kindness, and realized then that the majority of the nicest and most accepting people I met in my short life were Jewish. I decided to follow that thought and vowed to learn more about Judaism. But first I had to figure out a way to earn more money; I was running out of stamps.

Arturo and Anita's money was for them, *nothing for my son,* was Arturo's motto which I heard over and over again through my adult life. I expected nothing more. I assumed Arturo was angry at his father, and since no one gave him anything he didn't earn, that should be my lot in life as well. Christmas was ten dollars—five dollars from Anita and five dollars from Arturo, and I was to be most grateful. Occasionally there were coins on the floor.

Lonely and bored one Sunday, I wandered through a flea market downtown where I found a treasure trove of Baccarat, Lalique, Waterford, Wedgewood and Limoge pieces grossly underpriced. I bought as much as I could hold and headed home excited and bursting with pride. I showed the pieces to Arturo who systematically tapped them with his knuckle for the sound, an indication of quality. He checked each piece with a magnifying glass and made sure the seals and etched logos were authentic.

He smiled and said, "You remember. You did well." What are you going to do with them?"

"Resell them at great profit, Papa, come with me next week." I was hoping we could work together. He was the master.

"No, this conversation is over," he responded.

I was gravely disappointed. I thought it was a missed opportunity. So I decided to pursue it on my own, and week after week I visited every flea market, antique store, street fair, estate sale and auction, as much as time and money would allow, and bought and sold items I knew about. I met interesting collectors and dealers, and networked in a world I was unaware existed. From my study and collecting of stamps—known as *philately,* I moved to studying and collecting vintage postcards— called *deltiology.* Also, because of the geography that I learned through collecting stamps, I began to study and collect maps—known as *cartography,* as well as autograph collecting—known as *philography*. I was introduced to the wide world of collectors of paper—known as *ephemera*, which includes trade cards, greeting cards, and particularly holiday cards. Blue Santas were, and I assume still are, rare. I collected book marks, letters, pamphlets, posters, prospectuses—mainly items that were transitory.

While I engaged in these activities to earn extra money, I was also a collector. And as a collector, for me the thrill was in finding, acquiring and ultimately enjoying whatever item(s) peaked my interest. My real love was *horology*, the study and measurement of time which led me to collecting, buying and selling vintage wristwatches, table clocks and military instruments. I was not only building knowledge but a library of reference books, price catalogues, etc., all kept under the couch after late night reading.

None of this served my social life well, but it did help me to build and pursue my dream of being in my own business, buying and selling antiques and collectibles as I chose. I simply wasn't earning enough to justify starting a business

Dating was a challenge. I had no trouble meeting women when I ventured out, but I wasn't happy with the constant questions, mostly what do you do, meaning, how much are you worth? Stating I was a shoe salesman caused many women to excuse themselves early, develop emergencies or headaches, and basically dismiss me. Stating I was an antique dealer, philatelist or horologist was a little more appealing, but living with mom and dad, well, that was a relationship killer. Coming from Cuba frightened many as they associated Cubans as communists and we were still in a Cold War. If I said my grandparents came from Spain which they did on both sides, and that I lived there before I came to America, that was acceptable. I simply was not good husband material, and basically that was all that was wanted—at least from the women I was meeting. I desperately needed my own place.

. . .

JANUARY, 1974
STARTING OVER

By the time I was twenty-eight, I had a sense of well-being. I earned enough to support myself, rid my history of my first marriage, and was eager to move on with life. Leroy the manager of the very first shoe store where I worked, was doing well as an actor, and had to be in California for a television series; his first big break. He sublet his tiny studio apartment to me on the West Side of Manhattan, in a large apartment building with a dentist and a pharmacy on street level. It was most convenient for me.

I was amused by the ladies clothes I found in the apartment and figured he was too rushed to return them to his girlfriend of the moment, so I packed them away and kept them for him. Leroy had several girlfriends over the years. He loved women. Unfortunately, he loved many women. He just didn't date them, he studied them. When he had learned all he needed to know about each one, he moved on to the next. I was fascinated and wondered why he couldn't just stick with one. Perhaps because his dream of show business took precedent over his need to be with one woman. Women loved him. He was kind, quirky, and eager to experiment with everything. He was far more adventurous than I. He had broken several hearts I am sure. I wished him luck in California, and hoped he would have fun along with the success he craved.

I promised to take good care of his apartment, and was eager to hear about his adventures in show business. I was free, and I experienced that feeling of calm delight. I loved the neighborhood, vibrant and convenient, and I became quite health conscious and joined a gym; ladies on the second floor, men on the first. I remember smiling as I worked out, sure that something good was to happen. I watched my diet and became vegetarian. I was happy, busy and hopeful towards the future.

As I was again going to the bakery on the East side, there was a long line of customers, so I joined the line and stood behind a young woman in a business suit. She was particularly noticeable because of her unique glasses and the well-worn briefcase she carried. I also noticed she did not have a coat and wondered if she was cold or dressed in layers as I had done. As the line moved toward the front, I scoped out slices of chocolate babka, my favorite. Unfortunately, people were buying them by the slice, and by the time the young woman in front of me reached the counter, there were only two left.

"'ll take those two slices of chocolate babka," she said.

I groaned and said under my breath, "Oh no."

That pretty, kind lady turned to look at me, smiled sweetly and said, "Save them for him, I'll take the chocolate muffin on the left." She paid and began to leave. As she walked towards the door, she turned, smiled again and said, "Have an easy day."

I saw it as a simple act of kindness. There had been so few in my life, that I treasured each and every one as a special memory. Embarrassed but grateful, I attempted to thank her but the people on line were in a hurry and demanded I put in my order with remarks like, "Oh, c'mon buddy;" "Let's go;" "I'm not getting any younger."

One must move quickly in New York. I bought the remaining babka, paid, ran out the door to see if I could find her. I had a glimpse of her profile as she entered a bus heading uptown. She was gone but she seemed familiar. I noticed the magnificent structure across the street. It was a synagogue. I stood outside for a long time, admiring the building, when a young rabbi named Levy came up to me and asked if he could be of help. Embarrassed, I blurted, "I would love to see the inside, but I am not Jewish."

Rabbi Levy invited me in and showed me around. It was impressive. I sat across from him in his small office. He offered me a cup of tea; we shared a piece of chocolate babka. I felt at peace. We talked about life.

He said, "In our studies we learn that it is our duty to find ourselves a teacher and a friend."

I told the Rabbi that I thought Benjamin, Ruth and Irene were teachers and that Stanley was a friend. I missed them all. Rabbi Levy was reassuring when he explained that people often pass through our lives for a reason. We must figure out why and grow from there. I asked if he thought it was wrong for me to feel so comfortable with people of different faiths. On the contrary, he explained, it was a noble soul who accepts and respects all people. Then he sent me home with books to read about the

Jewish faith, and invited me for tea the following week. I tried to discuss all of this with my parents; they were indifferent.

After several weeks of meetings with Rabbi Levy, where we discussed everything from religion to politics, I decided to make the commitment and go through a conversion. First I had to appear before a panel of three rabbis, one of whom was Rabbi Levy. He asked me what I was searching for. I told him and the other rabbis something like, a religion which prepares me for life, as opposed to my religion which was preparing me for the afterlife, and where my life was more important than my soul.

That was a worthy distinction for me. I needed something to cling to during my lifetime; I wanted to celebrate life, I wanted my life to mean something to others. I wanted to love and be loved.

Rabbi Levy informed me that I would have to fulfill certain requirements, such as gaining knowledge of Hebrew, Jewish history and culture; experiencing and observing holidays, etc. I agreed to attend classes and began my studies diligently; classes were in the evenings three times per week. There were students of various ages and backgrounds and I was happy to be part of it. I did well and never missed an opportunity to visit the bakery across the street.

After several months of study, I fulfilled all the requirements and was officially converted. At the following Friday night services, I was introduced by Rabbi Levy as the newest member of the congregation. A couple in their forties paid particular attention to me as I stood in front of the congregation, and were engaging in intense whispering.

During the Rabbi's speech, he waivered and said, "Yes, Mrs. Viperman, he is single. Julian is special in that he chose to join us in our faith of good deeds, and our passion to improve the world we live in. He has studied our history, culture, language and traditions. We welcome him, and look forward to many years of friendship."

I was proud of the person I was becoming.

At the Oneg Shabbat—*Sabbath Joy*, where food and drink are served after the services, I met many of the congregants. Dr. and Mrs. Viperman, apparently wealthy, stylish, and gregarious, approached and announced that they arranged a dinner in my honor the following Saturday night. I was impressed and humbled.

"You are one of us now," cooed Mrs. Viperman.

Dr. Viperman handed me his business card. The Park Avenue address looked familiar. As Dr. and Mrs. Viperman left, I heard Mrs. Viperman say, "What a gift!" I wasn't quite sure what that meant or even if was directed towards me. I'd soon find out.

The following Saturday night I arrived at the Park Avenue address. The building, vast and elegant, looked familiar. I waited while the doorman checked with the Viperman's. Just then an elevator opened and emergency personnel wheeled out a stretcher with Madame on it.

Who could forget Madame, the lady who tried to steal my father's third package? She still made me nervous. She sat up abruptly, pointed an arthritic finger at me and screamed, "You, those gold coins were for my grandson!"

The Doorman was apologetic, "So sorry sir, please ignore her. She is very sick in the head. She only gets one channel, know what I mean?"

He twirled his finger by his ear, the universal symbol for 'crazy'. "Your name is on the list; take the elevator on the right to the fourth floor."

A bit shaken, I was welcomed by a maid, and joined Rabbi Levy and Dr. and Mrs. Viperman for cocktails. A few minutes later their twenty-eight year old daughter, Tiffanie Simone, a direct opposite of Mrs. Viperman in manner, attire and class, joined us. She walked like John Wayne, wore no makeup, dressed in drab colors and was frankly plain and plump.

Dinner was elegant. As expected there were a lot of questions about my family and me. I told them I sold shoes and recently became a vegetarian. At that point, Tiffanie joined the conversation and sarcastically asked her mother, "A shoe salesman? Mother, what will everyone think?"

It was more of a swipe against her mother than me, but I didn't appreciate it. Dr. Viperman quickly answered for his wife, "A discount, probably." Then he continued, "Now, Julian, how long have you been a vegetarian?"

Smooth move. I answered him and asked if he agreed that good nutrition and exercise, along with oxygen and water, are basic needs for life.

"I would agree, but I am still not convinced that vegetarianism is the way to go," he said.

Mrs. Viperman ended that conversation, "Enough shop talk. We are disappointed your parents couldn't make it."

"They have an early flight to Spain," I lied.

"Ooh, how exciting. Tell us about Madrid." I gave a quick tour of Madrid, and made a hasty departure with the excuse that I had to help my parents prepare for their trip. Tiffanie walked me to the door.

"You understand, I don't care what you do. You are a nice guy, right?" she said.

I nodded, "Apology accepted. Obviously they are trying to fix us up," I answered.

"They're desperate to get me married so I can be 'normal' she replied.

"Don't you think you should tell them you are not interested in men?" I asked.

She slapped me on the back, "See? You just met me and figured it out. They've known me for twenty-eight years and don't have a clue," she smiled.

"Tiffanie Simone, what will everyone think?" I mimicked her. We both laughed and said good-bye. That building had bad vibes for me. I needed to walk.

There was a club down the street from Leroy's apartment where people of all backgrounds met and discussed human values and current events. I attended meetings from time to time, always on the lookout for *miss right*. As I left for the club one night, I could have sworn I saw a pretty woman who seemed familiar, leave the dentist's office. Was it the glasses? Should I speak to her? As I got closer, I saw her holding gauze against her mouth. She must have had a procedure, so I thought it better not to bother her, but I wondered who she was, and why she seemed familiar. There were a million women in New York, but this one affected me in ways I couldn't explain or understand at the time.

A few days later Dr. Viperman called and asked me to meet him at Central Park's jewel of a restaurant, Tavern on the Green, for cocktails. I asked him why and he insisted it was important.

It was one of the most beautiful restaurants I have ever seen and one I could only hope to afford to eat dinner at some day. After drinks, he told me how much he admired me. He then asked me if I had ever been so in love with someone that I would do anything to make them happy.

I had no idea where he was going with his conversation, but I told him that I had been in love and at the time felt the same.

"Then you will understand what I am about to ask you to do." I didn't like the sound of that and prepared to excuse myself and to offer to pay for my drink, but he continued, "Mrs. Viperman is dying." He began to weep quietly. I felt horrible.

"I'm so sorry," I said earnestly.

"She's not expected to live beyond six months." I was speechless. I had no idea what he was expecting me to do. I listened. "The only thing my wife wants is for Tiffanie to be happy and married." I was being manipulated, I thought, and stifled a giggle. Before I could respond, he raised his hand and said. "I know she's gay, Julian, and I know you know. Tiffanie told me. Would you pretend for a little while that you are interested in my daughter so that when the time comes for Mrs. Viperman to leave us, she can go in peace? It would mean so much to her—and to me. My heart is broken, if I could just see her happy, I would be so grateful."

Was he offering me money? I was insulted. I remembered my lessons about good deeds. I needed to think this through. I promised to think about it. We ordered another drink. He told me about his work as a heart specialist and lamented about how ironic it was that he could save so many lives except the one most important to him. I again reassured him I would consider his request, and we changed the topic, and spoke about politics, antiques and fine wines. He seemed to be a decent man; concerned about humanity. He listened to what I had to say, was respectful, and made me feel good.

The following week I accompanied the Viperman family to a member's only country club, where Dr. Viperman introduced me to golf. We had a full and active day. I watched Mrs. Viperman flit from table to table and bubble over with animated conversation. She proudly introduced me to staff and members. I was dazzled by the attention. It was a fun day.

Over the next few weeks, Tiffanie and I became friends; we shopped and I introduced her to more suitable clothing and accessories that highlighted her attributes. Mrs. Viperman was delighted.

Tiffanie enjoyed her makeover. We often laughed about competing for the same women, and enjoyed a mutually respectful friendship. I was included in dinners and parties, and introduced to a luxurious life one only saw in movies. Mrs. Viperman was an elegant, well-bred woman, who made everyone feel welcomed and important. But she was failing. Her energy was waning, her ability to keep up with conversation was challenged, and she started to spend more and more time in bed. She filled her head with details of an imagined wedding for Tiffanie, and that seemed to calm her when she started becoming anxious. Within a short time, she succumbed to the cancer that ravaged her body. The funeral was an event attended by many friends, family and colleagues. It was my first funeral, and I wondered if Mrs. Viperman became an angel like my childhood friend Angelo.

I continued my friendship with Dr. Viperman and Tiffanie. They were grateful for my part in making Mrs. Viperman's remaining time hopeful. We've enjoyed several dinners over the years. They both promised to be available to me if the need ever rose. Dr. Viperman kept his promise many years later.

I continued my collecting, and occasional buying and selling. Dating was becoming a chore. I had several 'blind dates' through members of the Synagogue, none of which led to a relationship, but I enjoyed living alone in the studio apartment.

Then came the rumors that the shoe store would be closing. Stock was not being replenished in a timely manner, so I needed a new plan. In the meanwhile, I worked steadily and continued my routine. One day I was working with a spoiled, rich, middle aged woman. She had already tried on a dozen pair of shoes; they were strewn about.

"Let me try those lizard boots just for the fun of it," she insisted.

I started collecting the shoes and said casually, "Which of these may I ring up?"

She coiled like a snake, "I'll let you know," she sneered.

I sat on the stool, kept my patience in check, and asked if she wanted to see anything else. "Maybe," she teased.

Then she spread her legs and placed her foot on my crotch. I slipped off the stool. She just laughed and said, "Is that all you dear?"

I walked away and said, "I'll get the manager for you."

She quickly responded, "No need, play time is over. I'll take one pair of the sale shoes." She picked up the box she wanted and followed me to the counter.

"Cash or charge?" I asked.

She emptied the contents of her bag all over the counter and complained, "I can't seem to find my credit card." Eventually she did and finally paid. "Commission isn't all it's cracked up to be, is it?" she noted. I was tired of those types of women.

I went out after work to a sophisticated lounge. A young, sharp-eyed, and eared, bartender worked the crowded bar. While I stood at the bar, a well-dressed attractive woman brushed my arm and wiggled close to me.

"Good evening, may I buy you a drink?" I asked in my best Cary Grant manner.

"Sure handsome, love your accent."

I motioned to the bartender and he came over. "I'll have a gin and tonic and the young lady will have..." I pointed to her.

She answered, "A white wine spritzer."

The bartender said, "Coming right up."

He stayed within earshot. The young woman just looked at me and said, "Cindy, thirty, single, libra. I teach special ed."

I toasted her and said, "Julian, thirty, single, capricorn."

"What do you do, Julian?"

"I'm a shoe salesman, Cindy."

Cindy gulped down her drink and said, "Oops, it's late, excuse me."

The bartender placed a refill in front of me and said, "This one's on me, buddy."

Between the women customers and the women I was meeting to date, I was feeling a bit depressed. I visited Rabbi Levy. Over pastries and tea we talked about the end of the Viet Nam War, the new T.V. program *Saturday Night Live*, and the movie *Godfather II*, in which the character of Michael Corleone expands his criminal enterprises from Lake Tahoe in Nevada, and then to pre revolution 1958 Cuba. The scenes that included Castro's takeover brought back memories; people were talking about Castro again. I just wasn't happy.

Rabbi Levy said, "I sense a deep need in you."

I said, "There have been too many good-byes. I need to be special to someone; accepted and respected, and I want to feel the same about her."

"Ahh, love, Julian. Love is a worthy pursuit. When it's time, Julian, when it's time," he assured me.

. . .

JUNE, 1976
NEW YORK CITY

Soon after my thirty-first birthday, the store closed. I refocused my efforts on my knowledge of antiques. I started to attend trade shows where I could buy and sell, so I needed a resale number. I had that sense of calm delight as I headed downtown to fill out my application. I was about to take my first step in seeing my dream become a reality. As I entered and moved quickly through the revolving door of the building where I had to get the application, a very pretty lady with glasses and a briefcase exited. She seemed familiar. Once I realized who it was, I tried unsuccessfully to catch up with her. She walked swiftly and the herds of people prevented me from reaching her. I caught a glimpse of her as she disappeared down the steps to the subway heading uptown. Serendipity?

I still needed a full time job so I reluctantly called Frank, my uncle's customer who was the district manager of the chain of shoe stores where Leroy and I had previously worked. He was happy to hear from me and eager to have me back in the company—and apologized for not helping me the day I was robbed. Because of that incident, the company put extra security measures in place in every store, and he wanted to know where he could reach Leroy. The chain was opening a new store in mid-town, women's shoes only, and wouldn't it be wonderful if Leroy and I would co-manage? I said I would contact Leroy and let him know.

Leroy was thrilled to hear from me. Things in California were not going well; he had given it three years, was gravely disappointed, and decided to leave L.A. He was on his way back to New York, so I had to give up the apartment. He was eager to work steadily again. We discussed the new store and decided we had enough leverage to ask for decent salaries. What we didn't know was that we had to join a union, and salaries were by union contract. I called Frank and told him Leroy and I would return as a team if we had input into the styles to be sold. Frank was agreeable, and I was feeling pretty good about myself until I packed my suitcases and again, stood in front of my parent's building. After a few minutes I hoisted my belongings and went into the apartment. Nothing had changed except there were more lamps and small chandeliers in every room.

The next morning I prepared for work and noticed the shower had a very narrow stream of water coming out of the shower head. I complained to my parents. They hushed me quickly; terrified to say anything to the landlord. How long had they lived with the broken shower?

Against their protestations, I sent a certified letter to the landlord and asked that the shower be repaired, which it was within the week. My parents went through severe anxiety fearing they would be evicted. They just never bothered to know their rights. After that incident, I made sure to check on them very closely.

I hated living with them. My parents hadn't changed in any way, and were very difficult to deal with. I had little savings after living on my own, and was grateful to not have to pay full rent. I still dreamed of having my own business, so I made the best of it and kept busy.

A year went by and I was thirty-two; fit and happy despite moving back in with my parents. Leroy and I fell back into a comfortable work environment. The store was larger than the one in The Bronx, and the neighborhood was far better, the customers sharper and more demanding. We had four salespeople under us, along with a cashier and a maintenance guy. Leroy left most of the management to me. He was trying to reawaken his stalled show business career, and I was eager to rise in the company.

Our customer base consisted mainly of women who were middle aged, retired, secretaries, and office clerks. I kept fashion magazines in the store so that everyone was up on the latest fashion in color and style. We sold accessories like handbags, belts, and hosiery; the store did well. Despite living with Anita and Arturo, I again had that feeling of calm delight—that always predicted something good happening.

Managing the store took most of my time. My days off, which were rare, were devoted to my various hobbies. When I had time, I looked for an apartment. I was in no hurry since I was rarely at home, and I was finally able to save some money again.

Two years later, Leroy and I were doing well. We worked hard and partied occasionally, though I still hadn't found love. Leroy was still working on his show biz career and one night asked me to meet him at a singles bar. I thought it unusual, but agreed and went out to meet him. A lot of questions followed from Anita and Arturo. I told them I had a business emergency, and assured them I would call at nine o'clock, which I did. I entered the bar but I didn't see Leroy. It was a dark place so I took a seat at the bar, ordered a drink, and waited. An attractive woman sat next to me and said in a strange voice.

"Thanks for coming, Julian." I thought it was a joke. I looked closer. She looked familiar but it was hard to tell.

Just then a deep baritone voice came out of the woman and said, "Don't freak on me, man. It's Leroy." Leroy was a transvestite.

Those clothes I found in his apartment were his! I was stunned. I partied with this guy, he loved women. I had a million questions. We stayed up much of the night confessing to each other. At thirty-three I felt old and constantly challenged by life. By the next day, I had a splitting headache; I needed to work out. I finished late and went to the gym where the only place men and women were in the same space was by the swimming pool. As I entered for a swim, there was the same pretty woman with the nice figure that I had previously seen leaving the pool. She put on a pair of glasses.

By the time I realized who she was, she wrapped herself in a towel and went to the women's lockers. I asked the manager for her name, and he said she was a regular, but the rules forbade him from giving out information about members. At least I knew she was a regular, I made note of the time, and went back to the pool and swam away my headache. That woman was beginning to haunt me. Now that I had seen her several times, I needed to talk to her, to get to know her, to touch her.

That night I had a flying dream. I woke up thinking about her. I returned to the gym several times at the same time of day hoping to see her. Unbeknownst to me, she had given up her membership.

• • •

AUGUST, 1979
WEDNESDAYS LOUNGE, NYC

It was Wednesday. I was closing up the store and noticed a newspaper someone had left behind. I picked it up to discard in the trash, and that feeling of calm delight came over me. I sat down to read it through. It included a list of events for singles. There was an event that night at a place called Wednesdays, located near my favorite vegetarian restaurant. I read it twice and thought *why not go to Wednesdays on a Wednesday?*

It was a beautiful summer evening in Manhattan. People were out and about. The mood was light; there was music in the street. I had a light dinner and was eager to go to the event. I walked the few blocks to Wednesdays and noticed several men standing outside ogling the women who entered mostly in groups. I walked in; there was a long bar up front where several people gathered. As if I had wings, I glided toward the back of the long hallway filled with booths and scattered tables around a dance floor.

There she was again, the woman I wanted desperately to know. I increased my stride. She didn't see me but a redhead across from her did—and she smiled at me, and held that smile until I approached the table. I introduced myself. "Good evening ladies, I'm Julian." The redhead's *stuck on smile* was mute. I looked directly at the one I wanted to meet—she took the lead.

"Hello Julian," she said, "I'm Lynn."

I liked the sound of her voice; I liked her name; I liked her manners. She directed me to the smiling redhead and said; "Meet Sally." I nodded while Sally grunted, and in a deep smoker's voice she said, "Sal, call me Sal."

Sal had two drinks in front of her. She sipped loudly on her half-filled drink while Lynn continued, "Why don't you join us?" I was thrilled at the invitation.

"Thank you," I said.

"Here, sit next to Sally," she urged. I did as she suggested, then Lynn turned her whole body away from us and focused on the dance floor. Did I miss something?

Sal, (*call me Sal*) tried to make sophisticated chatter as she slurped her way through to the next drink, and while Lynn watched the dancers. Why wasn't Lynn paying attention to me? She wasn't rude; it was as if she did her duty and placed me with Sally where I belonged. After an agonizing twenty minutes of nonsense, Sally excused herself and went to the ladies' room. I took the opportunity to move closer to Lynn. Boldly I took her hand, her soft, delicate hand, with long beautifully manicured nails and said "I will dance with your girlfriend if that is what you want me to do, but it is your telephone number I want."

Lynn blushed and smiled. Sally returned to the table noticed I had changed my seat and said, "It's about time. Sorry buddy you're just not my type, have fun you two." She made a beeline for a tall man standing alone in the corner.

Finally, Lynn and I were alone. I asked her to dance; we fell into each other's arms and floated to the music, silently at first. She looked at me directly and said "Have we met before? You seem so familiar."

"No," I answered, but I believe we've seen each other before— several times. There was so much to talk about. "Why did you sit me next to Sally?" I asked.

"She saw you first and laid claim. It would have been disrespectful of me to show an interest. It's the girlfriend code, an unspoken rule between women."

Just then, Sally broke in to say goodnight, she was going to leave with her new, tall friend. Lynn and I continued to dance. We discovered that we worked in the same neighborhood, lived near each other at the time I sublet Leroy's apartment, and yes, she had gone to the dentist in Leroy's building. We belonged to the same gym, shopped in the same stores—why hadn't we ever met each other before?

I asked her for a date for Saturday night and she agreed. She gave me her contact information and I promised to call her. She laughed and said, "I hope you won't stand me up too."

Confused, I asked her to explain. She told me she had originally planned to go to The Hamptons for the Labor Day weekend, and stay with her friends Richard and his artist companion, Andres. She was scheduled to leave the next morning, Thursday. However, at the last minute, the trip was cancelled. It seemed Richard and Andres were having relationship issues. At first she was disappointed, but was glad Sally invited her to Wednesdays. Since I knew she was free the whole weekend, I suggested we spend it together.

"Let's take it slow." she said, but agreed to dinner the following evening, Thursday.

Had Richard not cancelled, Lynn would never have gone out Wednesday night and we would not have met. Lynn and I are forever grateful to Richard for cancelling, and have enjoyed many years of friendship with him and Andres. Sadly, Andres died from AIDS complications, and Richard moved to Nashville with his new companion, Jim, and we remain friends until this day.

We continued to get to know each other and I discovered she had never been married; she lived alone in a co-op apartment on the West Side of Manhattan, and worked as an executive assistant directly across from the United Nations Building. I was impressed with Lynn, and didn't want anything to harm what I hoped to be a growing relationship. Therefore, I did not tell her I was selling shoes, but was an antique dealer, and could not be reached during the day because I shopped for the business. I did not tell her I was from Cuba, but that I lived in Spain before I came to America.

It was getting late and time to go. It must have been about 10:30 by then. The strangest thing happened. As we walked through the long hallway of Wednesdays, hand in hand, the crowd of singles parted like the Red Sea and stood aside respectfully as we exited. We both were touched and a bit confused by the collective gesture and never forgot the night we met.

We shared a taxi across town; she let me off by the subway and we waived at each other until we both disappeared from each other's sight.

• • •

SEPTEMBER, 1979
PARENTS' APARTMENT

I was enthralled and eager to get home to rest up for Thursday night. I walked into the apartment, and there was Anita and Arturo huddled by the door waiting for me. They looked grim. My mood fell and matched theirs. "Who died?" I asked.

"No one, your mother promised her sister Marta she could get her out of Cuba so she could live with us. See to it!"

"Where is she going to sleep?" I inquired, this apartment is too small."

"It's cheap and it's perfect," my father replied.

"You'll sleep with your father on the couch, and Marta and I will have the bedroom," my mother chimed in.

"Ridiculous!" I said, "I'm going to bed."

"Call *Cara De Luna*," shouted my father.

"My pock marked friend's name is Badilla. Call him Badilla!"

"Don't talk to your father like that, just do what he says!" Anita lamented. I was tired.

"I'll take care of it, please go to sleep!"

They kept issuing orders and chattering. Somehow I shut them out, curled up on the couch and fell into a deep sleep dreaming about Lynn. The next day I arranged to have lunch with Badilla and told him of my newest dilemma. Could he arrange for my Aunt Marta to stay with any of his contacts in Mexico? He promised to make a call and get back to me.

. . .

Thursday morning, before Lynn and I were to meet, Sally called her to find out what happened with me. Lynn told her I was coming over. Sally made the following two suggestions.

1. Leave the toilet seat up so I would feel jealous, thinking there was another man in Lynn's life.
2. Spray perfume on colored bulbs around the house to set the mood.

Lynn laughed off the toilet seat suggestion, thinking it was foolish, but was willing to try the perfumed bulb proposal. After my three o'clock phone call, she went shopping for goodies for the evening. She purchased a blue bulb to place in her living room. She had a couple of hours before I was due to arrive so she placed the blue light bulb in the lamp, curled up on the couch with a good book, and read by the blue light.

Sally neglected to explain that perfume should not be sprayed on a hot light bulb. Shortly before I was to arrive, Lynn followed Sally's instructions and sprayed perfume on the bulb. It immediately began to smoke. By the time I arrived, flowers in hand, Lynn was busy airing out her apartment, and trying desperately to clear the smoke from the living room.

We had a good laugh about it, and when the smoke cleared, I helped her serve the hors d'oeuvres she prepared. I was impressed; she showed class and good manners, and I hoped I did the same. We talked well into the night and continued to get to know each other. We were interested in each other's lives; she was so easy to talk to. While we both wanted more, we knew something special was happening.

After Lynn's weekend plans had changed, we decided to spend the Labor Day weekend together. She asked me what I wanted to do and I mentioned a science fiction movie being shown in Greenwich Village. I asked her what she wanted to do and she told me she wanted to see the movie *Apocalypse Now.* So before I left, I gave her money for reserved seats, which she promised to pick up on the way to the hospital in Yonkers where she was going to visit a sick relative.

I went home that Thursday night even happier than I was the night before when we first met. I wasn't scheduled to see her until Saturday night, but I wanted to speak with her so I called Friday night after I returned from work. We spoke by phone for about two hours, which did not go unnoticed by Anita and Arturo.

Saturday, I worked all day and was eager for the day to end so I could see Lynn. From the hallway, as I approached her apartment, I heard soft music playing. When I arrived with a box of chocolates and an overnight bag, she thanked me for the candy and didn't say anything about my overnight bag. I didn't want her to think I was being presumptuous, so I explained that I worked all day and brought a change of clothes for dinner. She smiled, which made me feel comfortable.

We talked about the weekend, and she told me she bought the movie tickets for Monday, Labor Day afternoon. It took a moment for that to sink in. I realized the change of clothes was a good idea. I smiled.

She prepared light refreshments before we went to dinner. While I freshened up in the bathroom, I found a child's blue toothbrush. She told me she had never been married. My stomach began to hurt.

I looked around the neat, but sparsely furnished one-bedroom apartment, and didn't see any evidence of a child until she suggested I place my overnight bag in the front coat closet. There was her old beaten up briefcase. I placed my bag next to it and saw a stack of puzzles and boy toys. I didn't say anything.

Whatever anxiety I was beginning to feel melted when over dinner she told me about her family and the men in her life; her brother and two nephews, whom she adored. The oldest nephew was three years old, and the baby was just born. The little blue toothbrush was from a recent visit from her nephew.

She was born and raised in Brooklyn, attended Samuel J. Tilden High School, as did her dad and other relatives, and Brooklyn College at night. Her dad had died in 1966 at a very young age, and her mother lived in Florida where there were several other relatives, including her aunts, uncles, and cousins. She also had second cousins and a great aunt and uncle from her father's side living in her building.

It was a beautiful summer evening, so after dinner we took a long walk, continued our conversation, and bumped into friends of hers who had just had a baby girl the month before. She had many friends. I admired the fact that she kept her family and friends close. My friends were limited, and my family—how was I going to bring this lovely woman into my circle of dysfunction?

My thoughts went to my Aunt Marta. How was I going to manage the task of getting her to the U.S.? I must have zoned out for a minute or two. Lynn asked me if I was alright. She touched me gently, and I was fine.

She asked me to wait while she went into a food store. She came out with two bags, a large one for us and a smaller one for a homeless person who I didn't even notice. She handed him the food and said "Have an easy night." She then bought the *Sunday Times*. She turned her attention to me, slipped her arm through mine and said, "Let's go home." We were becoming partners. We embraced and took a long bus ride to her apartment. We noticed our reflections in the window opposite us, looked at each other and smiled. We knew we were moving forward with our relationship, and we needed nothing to 'set the mood' except each other.

Feeling comfortable, I placed my wallet, keys and a shoehorn on her dresser. I left the shoehorn there. She noticed it and didn't say anything. After a romantic Sunday morning breakfast, we were off to an adventure in Greenwich Village, a colorful energetic part of Manhattan. We attended a science fiction retrospective event at a quaint theater, had lunch and dinner at fun restaurants, and enjoyed the sights and sounds of another beautiful summer evening in Manhattan.

By Monday we were a little saddened that the weekend was coming to an end. We saw *Apocalypse Now*, and I noticed Lynn covered her eyes during the violent parts. I wrapped my arms around her and whispered, "It's only a movie." She appreciated that, though she still covers her eyes during violence in films.

"It offends my eyes," she says. After the movie, Lynn walked me to the subway and it was back to Spanish Harlem for me.

As soon as I returned home, I tried to call her. That did not sit well with my mother. I had been gone for the weekend so she thought she deserved my time and attention, and demanded we have a talk. So, before I finished dialing, I hung up and sat with my mother and father who for the first time I can remember, showed an interest in any of my girlfriends. They knew my feelings for Lynn were different and more serious than the others. They asked for details. Surprised but pleased, I was happy to comply and told them everything I knew about her.

"Lynn is my age and has never been married." I caught them looking at each other with skepticism. I continued, "She is independent and owns her co-op apartment." Papa didn't like that.

"Too mannish," he said.

She is smart and pretty and I am falling in love with her," I added. They sat quietly.

Then my mother said, "Why isn't she married?"

I responded, "Maybe she hasn't found the right one yet."

My mother wiggled her finger, "No, no, she's not normal."

My father agreed, "Your mother is right. She should be married by now. There is something wrong with her."

Sadly I found out later, Lynn's family felt the same way about her. I found her refreshing, and was glad she didn't bring an ex-husband or child to our relationship.

This may have been the first adult conversation I ever had with my parents.

"Those are old beliefs," I began, referring to women who are in the work force and independent, "in this country, if you don't follow old customs, and are ambitious it is not looked down upon as a betrayal to the family. I'm trying to blend the old with the new. Self-sufficiency is a beautiful thing. I am proud of what I accomplished, and if I am successful it is because you are my teachers. That doesn't mean I disrespect you or love you less. I will listen to you, Papa, because I put into practice everything I've learned from you." I had his attention.

"But my hope is to have a relationship with an equal partner that lasts as long as yours has. I've thought about your marriage and how you overcame difficulties."

"What are you talking about?" my father was probing.

I didn't want to talk about my mother's indiscretion, which I still thought he didn't know about. So I quickly responded. "Castro."

That monster," he replied, and I could see he was seething. I redirected the subject quickly.

"Look what you've been through, and how sturdy and strong your relationship is. That's what I want, a marriage like yours."

He calmed down, looked at my mother and embraced her. They held that embrace for a while. Despite their past, they were inseparable, they understood, accepted and enjoyed each other. They seemed to be a united team, and I honestly wanted a relationship like that. "Just know that I love you both dearly. And if Lynn is the right one for me I would like you to meet her, not for permission to be with her, but for your blessing."

Then I excused myself and called Lynn. We spoke for over an hour and made plans for the following weekend and, in my head, every weekend thereafter. Anita came in and out of the room several times trying to listen. Had she learned English it would have made her life easier. It would be awhile before I introduced Lynn to my family.

At the time we met, Lynn served on the board of directors of her reformed synagogue and was invited to serve because she helped create and implement weekly evening programs for a newly developed singles group. As we continued to date, she kept her commitment regarding the programming, but limited her attendance to business only, and eventually resigned her position.

We fell into each other's lives easily; Lynn introduced me to theater, museums, yoga and play. I didn't know how to play. I didn't know how to take a vacation. I didn't know how to relax. It bothered Lynn that I would stay dressed in my suit and tie until it was time for bed. I had no casual clothes.

I introduced her to the world of antiques and collectibles. She was a quick study, and learned how to recognize the difference between crystal and glass. She was of great assistance to me in my weekend shopping jaunts, and often accompanied me to trade shows. If I rented a table for selling, she manned the table, which allowed me the freedom to do more buying.

She had limited culinary skills. I taught her to cook vegetarian, meals and she enjoyed the creativity. She became a wonderful cook, and eventually we began to cook for each other.

She introduced me to casual clothes. I introduced her to thrift shops. She educated me in ways to make my money grow so I could focus on financial security and save for the future. I followed the Arturo Vida School of Finance, *trust no one and hide your cash*, and admittedly I was frugal. If I paid for dinner, there was no dessert. Lynn was more generous–if she paid, anything on the menu was fine with her.

Lynn's career consisted of working for successful executives. She learned how they made their money grow, and suggested I do the same within my comfort level, such as a mutual fund. She shared a formula she followed to have her money grow over the years; a combination of stocks, bonds, mutual funds and money markets. Although she had six months expenses in cash on hand, she had debt. She had to buy her co-op apartment. The only money she had was from a retirement fund, and which she had to put up as collateral. She had to borrow the remainder of the money from her great aunt and uncle who lived in the building.

It never bothered Lynn that her wealthy childless relatives who 'loved her like their own' charged her five and a half percent interest; she was grateful they cared enough to lend her the funds so she would have a place to live.

She celebrated life with every holiday, birthday and anniversary of friends, relatives and colleagues. She saved every greeting card she received, and her photos were precious to her. She kept them in boxes and enjoyed going through them, plucking out a photo every now and then. The photos she had around the house were of us, her mom, her brother and his family.

She was not religious, but spiritual. She believed there is more to us as humans than what we see in the mirror, and was a strong believer in energy—she believed everything has energy. If she bumped into a chair or other inanimate object, she apologized to that object—energy.

She was a good administrator, and helped me keep records of my business transactions. I focused on making the sale and moving on to the next customer. She awakened me to the importance of building relationships and following up. She had me order business cards and exchange them with new and established customers.

After months of dating, I continued my story about not being able to be reached during the day, and I made sure to keep in touch with her. One night I called her and she was disappointed.

"It's too bad I couldn't reach you today," she said, "my boss had two tickets available for a Broadway show." I felt badly; I knew it was one she was eager to see.

While Lynn and I were clearly a couple, and I spent most of my time at her apartment, I was eager to move from my parents' apartment and secure my own space. Lynn accompanied me as I looked for an apartment in Manhattan and Queens. I knew she wanted me to move in with her, and it made sense to do so, but I was unable to commit fully. My previous marriage left deeper scars than I thought. While I was committed to Lynn and our relationship, the possibility that it would fail and I would have to return to my parents and live with them again terrified me.

Lynn was unaware of my deep feelings about my previous marriage and my relationship with my parents, but seemed fully aware of my love for her. She rightfully told me that I seemed rigid and was giving her mixed signals about our future. Clearly frustrated with my inability to make a decision about where to live and/or marriage, she was right, and assured me she loved me and would do whatever I wanted; there was plenty of time and she was a patient woman.

Several months passed; I still hadn't told her I was Cuban, a converted Jew, and a shoe salesman. I made sure she hadn't met my folks, although I had already met many members of her family, and several friends. I had to open up to her but was so afraid of losing her. The pressure was building.

Around that time, when her boss moved on, she did as well. She found a new position as executive assistant to the chairman and president of a major restaurant chain. It was a demanding job. She left early for work, before I got up, and worked late. I continued to spend more time at her apartment, and we enjoyed the city as best we could, given our limited funds and long work hours. We were at the mercy of other people's schedules for lunch, vacation, days off, etc. We kept a hectic pace, worked hard, and did our best to balance work, play, and rest, even though I really did not know how to play—only to work.

Usually, Tuesday night was museum night. The museums opened to the public for free so we would meet after work, have a quick dinner and wander through those magnificent exhibits. Lynn's favorite was The Metropolitan Museum of Art. It was her sanctuary during colder months, as was Central Park during warmer weather.

. . .

Badilla called me; he had news about my Aunt Marta. He could get her to Spain. My parents sent her a one way ticket from Cuba to Spain, where she stayed at a rooming house with other Cubans eager to get to the United States. She went through the same process as I, and by Christmas of 1980 she was due to arrive in the United States.

CHAPTER THIRTEEN

DECEMBER, 1980
NEW YORK CITY, NY

I had to make a move quickly. Either locate an apartment or move in with Lynn. I was an emotional wreck. I knew I loved her, but was afraid of the commitment. It was time to tell her the truth about me. I would do it that night. I called her and asked if I could come over. She told me she was meeting with her family, so I offered to have dinner ready for her when she arrived home no matter how late it was. She was excited and agreed.

Unbeknownst to me, Lynn received a letter the day before from the board of directors of the building where she lived. There were internal wait lists for people hoping to move to two-bedroom and three-bedroom apartments.

Lynn's name came up as eligible for a two-bedroom apartment. The way I understood it, one did not own their apartment, but owned shares in a corporation, the number of shares represented by the size of an apartment. With approval from the board of directors, she would sell the one-bedroom apartment back to the co-op board, and use those funds plus an additional amount to purchase the shares representing the available two-bedroom apartment; she had to make a decision within a short period of time.

She planned to meet with her aunt and uncle that night to discuss the opportunity; she did not have the funds for the two-bedroom apartment. They refused to loan her the money, and told her that if she were to raise the money from another source, they wanted the balance of their loan to her paid first. They did not want her to carry two loans. Fortunately, one of her aunt's daughters, her second cousin, came to the rescue. She and her husband agreed to take money from their savings account, and loan it to her if she agreed to repay it at seven and one-half percent interest rate. Lynn agreed and was grateful to now own a two-bedroom apartment in Manhattan.

I prepared the meal and she was surprised and pleased. She was bubbling over with enthusiasm, but before she could give me her news, I asked her to sit because I had something urgent to tell her. She turned pale.

"Are you leaving me?" she asked. I grabbed her and kissed her.

"No, never, as long as you'll have me."

She brightened her demeanor, "Are you proposing marriage to me?" It was going all wrong.

"No, I just need to tell you something."

Her body collapsed, she seemed bewildered and deeply disappointed.

"I have not been totally honest with you." That touched a raw nerve. Her eyes slit. Remember Arturo's *silent stare*? The Lynn look is as deadly.

I knew I messed up. I was nervous and blurted out "I am not from Spain, I'm from Cuba. But I did live in Madrid before I came to the United States." Lynn was confused.

"What's the difference?" she asked.

"Too many people think Cubans are communists and illegals."

"Are *you*?" she inquired

"Which one, a communist or an illegal?"

"Pick one," she said.

"Neither, I hate Castro and what he stands for. My parents lost everything they had."

"I'm sorry." She was genuinely sympathetic.

"There's more," I continued. The slit narrowed.

"Go on," she challenged.

"I'm a converted Jew. My parents are Catholic." She sat straight and moved away from me.

"I must look very foolish to them. They must have been confused by the holiday cards I sent to them," she lamented.

"Everything confuses them," I answered. She was thinking now, rubbing her chin. It was a lot to absorb, especially after her family meeting.

"I'm not finished." My head hung low now. My voice softened. I was so ashamed. "I am a shoe salesman. I buy and sell antiques as a way of earning extra money."

Silence. I wondered if she could see through the slits. She stood up. "You must not have a high opinion of me if you don't think you can trust me with your truth," she said.

"I didn't want to lose you; I thought it was safer to lie." "You don't know me at all, Julian." I reached out and hugged her. She stiffened. I whispered, "The tighter you hold me, the freer I feel." I think you had better go home to your parents' house tonight. I have a lot to think about."

Crushed, I left and wept quietly all the way home.

• • •

Unbeknownst to me, Lynn called twice. My parents never learned how to take a message and I had begged them not to answer my phone, but they disconnected her both times and were too embarrassed to tell me. I was in agony. It was the weekend and I missed Lynn terribly.

I called her office first thing Monday morning; her secretary told me she was in a meeting so I left a number for her to call me at the shoe store; and just before closing, she returned my call and asked me to come by her apartment.

I flew to her building, flowers in hand. She was cool, but, as always, polite. While she prepared dinner I relaxed. "Are you ashamed of me, Julian?" she asked.

"Oh my God, no, I'm ashamed of me," I cried. She was pensive. I sat quietly. Finally, she spoke.

"There are no lies in love. Love is not position, power or money. Love is just love. Don't you understand that?" She took my hand and held it a long time. "I love you Julian, I don't care where you are from, or how you earn your money, as long as it is legal. And if there is no marriage, then I would be happy to spend whatever time I have with you, but I need to know I can trust you."

"You can," I stated.

"I understand why you lied and I know that you love me. The only request I have is that there be no more lies. It rattles the foundation of our relationship. Do you understand me?"

"Absolutely," I replied.

"Then remember, a promise not kept is also a lie," she added.

We talked well into the early morning and sealed our love with promises of mutual respect—and no more lies! I continued to spend time at Lynn's place, but did not move in permanently. We were both content with our arrangement.

CHAPTER FOURTEEN

December, 1980
NEW YORK CITY, NY

My Aunt Marta finally arrived. Despite her tiny frame—Marta was about four foot eleven and weighed about ninety pounds—she had a baritone voice. Oddly enough, her deep voice was a calming influence on my parents.

Arturo worked out a schedule with his boss to allow Anita and Marta to share cleaning chores. Each worked twenty hours per week. She cared nothing for money and sent much of what she earned to the remaining relatives in Cuba. Sometimes it arrived, sometimes not, but there was always a transaction fee. She contributed little to the household in funds, but took responsibility for the shopping, cooking and cleaning. She was not competitive in any way and was friendly to all.

Arturo, Anita and Marta shared food, gossip and often appeared to be on the same umbilical cord. They knew each other from childhood. Marta and Anita were raised down the block from where Arturo lived and worked in that antique store. Arturo was sixteen, Marta fourteen, and Anita twelve when they met. Marta was always the protector, eager to be of service to family and friends, and basically needed to be needed.

She was a single woman. She had a decades long relationship with a married seaman with a family; a lieutenant in the Navy. I remember him well, and was always saddened that they never established a secure relationship.

My father did not approve of their affair, and refused to give her a room in our house in Havana for fear she would become pregnant, and he would have another mouth to feed. He did, however, give her a rent free apartment in a building he owned. He put her in charge of collecting the rent, and had her keep an eye on the building. For her work he paid her a small monthly stipend, and he was happy not to know what went on in her apartment.

In a quiet moment between Aunt Marta and myself, she told me how proud she was of me. How amazed she was that given my history, I turned out so well, and she apologized for the beatings. The family knew, the neighbors knew, but the prevailing wisdom was to mind one's own business, and many people at that time in Havana feared my father.

Did her admission help me? No, those scars run quite deeply, but the acknowledgement was appreciated. At times, I thought no one knew or cared enough to protect me—especially my father. I was torn between my need for his love and attention, and anger at him for his total neglect.

Marta settled into the American way of life and was eager to assimilate. She encouraged my parents to learn English, so she and my father attended night classes. My mother was unable to keep up. Marta kept close ties to the family back in Cuba. They were struggling to survive, so Marta arranged with my parents to send most of her money to Cuba. My parents supported her; she in turn cooked and cleaned for them.

Marta told the relatives back in Cuba that I was doing well and suggested they call me if they needed help. Collect calls cost ten dollars per minute. One of my cousins called begging me for aspirin, band aids and any unused prescription medicines we had; and money—always money. That call cost me one-hundred and ten dollars. Free healthcare in Cuba is free only when it is available and if it is determined you are in need. Everything is rationed. A couple of weeks later, my uncle called to tell me that he, his wife and his daughter and her husband had one potato between them for dinner. Could I send them canned ham and money—*always money.*

The panic, stress and worry were taking an emotional toll on everyone. We needed a plan. After several family meetings between me, my parents and my aunt it was agreed that they would take care of those they could in Cuba; I would take care of my parents and my aunt.

About a week later my parents called me and asked me to stop by; they sounded calm. I left work feeling that we had resolved the issue with my Cuban relatives and looked forward to a pleasant evening. I arrived with food and as I walked down the hall to their apartment, I could hear excited chatter. They had company. When I entered, my parents and my aunt surrounded me by the door.

My mother said, "We have a surprise for you in the living room." She and Marta giggled.

"Alright you two, get to work," my father ordered and ushered the two women to the kitchen. He then excused himself and went into the bedroom and locked the door. I went to the dimly lit living room and in the corner I saw a small figure sitting in the chair grinning. As I moved closer, I noticed a bad wig and false teeth.

The bane of my existence, Rafael the policeman arose. No more muscle, no swift movement, just a fragile old man with arthritic hands. He attempted to hug me, I was rigid.

I grabbed him by the collar and whispered in his ear, "If you go near my mother I will rip your heart out with my bare hands." He backed away but showed no fear.

"Cool it kid, I'm just here to help your family and nothing else."

My father came into the room, and with a flourish handed Rafael an envelope that I assumed contained cash. "This should feed all of them for a few months. See to it." Rafael saluted. My father continued, "The women will prepare small packages filled with aspirin, mercurochrome, band-aids, etc. See they get to the right people."

Rafael saluted again. He had his instructions and I am sure he was paid well. "I gotta go," Rafael said. "Take care my friend." My father walked him to the door.

"Humph," my mother said, "at least he's good for something."

After he left I asked my parents how they found him. "We never lost touch," my father said.

. . .

While I still had not officially moved in with Lynn, I spent my time at her apartment. It was a year and a half from the time we met. The time was right for her to meet my family, so Lynn and I invited them to her apartment to share the Christmas holiday. Marta was unable to join us; she wasn't feeling well.

I offered to pick my parents up and bring them by taxi. They feared yellow taxis. "Why?" I asked.

With great authority they answered, "We will be kidnapped." I had no words. But, they knew a guy whom they assured me would deliver them safely; a neighbor who ran a Spanish speaking only car service—unregulated, unlicensed, uninsured, yet they felt perfectly safe. I let them be.

Christmas Day, 1980, they arrived, looked around—really looked around. They inspected the apartment as if it were a crime scene. They touched every piece of furniture, opened every cabinet and closet door. My father rapped everything he touched with his knuckles to determine its worth. Lynn watched in amazement as the two of them looked under her furniture. My mother went into her bedroom and looked through her closet. Lynn was surprised. I was embarrassed. After inspection we all gathered in the dining room and my father announced, "Mierda!" (shit!)

I was horrified. He then prattled on that there wasn't a piece of furniture worth a dime. I had to think fast. I was the interpreter. I told Lynn they were happy to meet her and looked forward to our time together, but Lynn is smarter than that—she didn't buy my interpretation. Then my mother immediately called Marta in order to gossip. They spoke for ten minutes. About every half hour after that, Anita called Marta again, with minute by minute updates. I told Lynn she wanted to brag about how happy I was.

Because it was Christmas Day, Lynn bought presents for them and prepared snacks and drinks. I neglected to tell her my family celebrated Christmas on January sixth. My parents were confused, Lynn was confused. I learned to sweat a lot.

Lynn set out a jigsaw puzzle for everyone to work on while we talked. My mother did well with the puzzle and loved the idea of play. We all celebrated each fitted piece with a shout of accomplishment. I interpreted like a diplomat. Lynn didn't know any Spanish, but was eager to learn. I asked her not to. When it was time to leave my father called his trusted neighbor for a pick up. Before my parents left, there were smiles and hugs all around. I felt hopeful.

In January, 1981, Marta suffered a heart attack. She was sixty-six years old and fragile. She was no longer able to work so my mother went back to work full-time while Marta stayed home, cooked and cleaned, and kept up relationships with neighbors.

In February, I officially moved into Lynn's two-bedroom apartment. We were thirty-six years old. We had great fun setting it up. She graciously set aside the second bedroom for my antiques and collectibles, and we made it an office. She took me to the bedroom and opened the clothes closet.

"I organize my clothes by color, thanks to you," she said, "short sleeve and long sleeve blouses, suits by season, skirts and slacks, sweaters on the shelves. My shoes are by heel height. The other side is yours."

I unpacked my suitcase and Lynn hung up my clothes. "I'll do the same," I said, "but all my shoes are flat." We laughed and hugged.

We moved to the living room where she had her bookcase. "My books are separated by law, literature, medicine and religion." She made space for my research books. Then she handed me a magazine holder and I filled it with antique, collectible and watch magazines. When we were finished I asked, "Any rules?"

"Neatness counts," she answered. We laughed again.

We continued unpacking my things. She was making room in a closet when she dropped her family photo box, the one with photos of her mom, dad and brother. Photos scattered, and as I helped her pick them up, I found her parent's wedding photo; I had never seen it before. I stared at it for a long time. Then casually, I said to her, "Your father looks like a younger version of a man I once knew. His name was Stanley."

She froze. I didn't think she was breathing. After a moment or two, she said, "How could you possibly know my father? He died in 1966."

I studied the photo again, more closely. Yes, it was he. I was overwhelmed and between my tears, I told her how we knew each other. We cried in each other's arms for hours. To this day, I weep every time I realize I fell in love with Stanley's daughter. I truly believe my relationship with Lynn is more than serendipity; it is born of miracles and sealed by fate!

There was no discussion of marriage or children. We were happy and busy working full time at our day jobs, and part-time at night and weekends on the collectibles and antique business.

Lynn introduced me to her accountant, made sure I had the proper tax I.D. number, set up my books, kept the records, paid my taxes, and handled my clients. I focused on the buying and selling.

Soon after Marta's recovery, Lynn prepared a Sunday family dinner for my parents and aunt to honor Marta's restored good health, and spent most of Saturday and Sunday morning preparing a sumptuous full meal starting with appetizers. I helped her set the table, placed fresh flowers in the center and we beamed with pride as we welcomed my family to our home.

They arrived with a plastic bag of fruit which was closed and knotted four times. We thanked them and guided them into the dining room. Arturo resisted. He refused to remove his coat or hat and stood by the door, arms folded like a sentinel. I had seen this stance recently and asked him what he was doing.

"Now I have two women to watch over," he said, "your mother and Marta."

"They're fine I assured him. Come, sit down Papa, relax."

"No!" he said. I left him alone. Anita and Marta removed their coats handed them to Lynn and made a bee-line for the bedroom chattering loudly in Spanish.

Believing they were looking for the bathroom, Lynn followed them, and was horrified that they were opening our drawers, going through our belongings, and diving through our closet like shoppers the day before Christmas.

She diplomatically led the ladies out of the bedroom, and offered them hors d'oeuvres. Food, they forgot about the bedroom, and filled their greedy little fists. They ate and rambled on as if nothing happened, completely unaware that they had offended Lynn. Lynn told me what she witnessed, and was appalled by their behavior. I spoke to them in Spanish, explained the situation and Anita replied, "So what? I always go through your things."

I had to interpret for Lynn, and was creatively putting a positive spin on what was being said. Lynn linked her arm through my father's and led him to a seat at the head of the table, helping him off with his coat. He resisted and announced in broken English, "I pass. We already ate!"

Lynn said to me. "Didn't you tell them they were invited for dinner?"

"Every night for a week," I said.

My father continued in broken English, "Not important. I eat my food."

Lynn was exasperated. I was embarrassed.

Anita came to the rescue, "I eat!"

She sat down at the table, pulled apart a piece of bread and held the dinner plate up to Lynn's face. "Food!" she demanded.

Lynn served her. Anita ate anything that didn't eat her. Her once svelte figure was expanding.

Marta sat at the table. She ate like a bird, but often. One had to serve her tiny amounts of food over and over. She thrust her dish in Lynn's direction and repeated, "Little, little, little."

I watched Lynn trot back and forth to the kitchen emptying and refilling dishes. It was dizzying.

Arturo with arms folded returned to his post by the door. They were maddening.

I tried to keep the peace. It was hard to keep up the pace of interpreting as they talked over each other in rapid-fire Spanish, and not always in a kind way. Arturo came back from his stance at the door and joined them for coffee, and when he was satisfied, placed his long arm over the table and Anita and Marta put their flatware down. The meal was over.

Lynn was about to sit down to eat when Arturo announced, "Women to kitchen, clean."

Like robots, Anita and Marta started to clear the table. Lynn insisted they not help, but as if they hadn't heard her they went about their business. They only took orders from Arturo. When Marta took a paper towel and started to clean the legs of the couch that was too much for Lynn. She physically stopped Marta, and asked her to sit and relax. After all, Marta had just recovered from a heart attack!

Arturo called his trusty car service, and waited to be picked up and delivered back to his apartment. He lit a cigar, finally relaxed. He was the king.

Lynn and I were exhausted. We had enough food left over for an army, and we barely ate, so Lynn called her friends from New Jersey and they and their two children were delighted to join us for a quiet dinner. At the end of the evening after everyone left, Lynn said, "No pressure, but if we ever do decide to marry, let's elope."

A few nights later Lynn and I had a romantic evening. The phone rang and rang. It was nine p.m. I answered. It was my mother.

"I'm in the middle of a personal moment," I told her.

"You're having sex?" she asked, "hold on, talk to your father. He has something important to ask you."

Lynn gave up and went to the kitchen. I heard the freezer door open. She loves her ice cream.

"Yes, Papa what is it?" I asked.

"How much did you sell today?"

The next evening, when the phone rang at nine, it went unanswered.

The following week was Lynn's thirty-seventh birthday. We had tickets for an evening performance at the Circle In The Square Theater. During intermission, I left my seat to call my mother. I did not hear the warning bell and by the time I headed back to my seat, the play had commenced. I walked through the curtain and actually bumped into an actor about to go on stage, which startled us both. As I reached my seat and looked to Lynn for forgiveness, her eyes slit and she crushed her program. I thought about running away. Terrified to move, I sat paralyzed in my seat, eyes forward.

Lynn did not speak to me the whole way home. We arrived at the apartment, and she busied herself by laying out her clothes for the next day, and preparing for bed. I couldn't stand the silence.

"Talk to me," I begged.

"Why do we have to organize our lives around the nightly nine o'clock phone call, she simply asked?

"Because my mother needs to hear my voice before she goes to sleep." I explained.

"I think *you* need to hear your mother's voice," she responded.

Then she went to bed; no conversation; no kiss goodnight. By morning, she was gone for work before I arose. I was in trouble.

I hadn't seen Rabbi Levy in a long time. He was no longer at the Synagogue, and the person I spoke to had no idea where he could be reached. I had no one to talk to. Then I realized that wasn't true. I could always talk to Lynn. She was my friend, my partner, my lover.

I asked her to join me for a quiet dinner out. She took my hand and said, "I would never do anything to come between you and your family."

"I know that," I responded.

"But must you speak to your parents every night?" she asked.

"What's the difference?" I said.

She continued, "Are you aware that given our work schedules, we see each other maybe twenty hours per week? And every night your nine o'clock phone call lasts between a half hour and an hour?"

"So," I said. She was soft and understanding.

"So, I don't understand Spanish, but the conversation sounds the same to me every night. Is it possible to speak to your parents during the day? And if it has to be at night, perhaps every other night?"

I didn't think there was anything odd about talking to my parents every night, and we did talk about the same thing over and over, but then again I tried to see it from Lynn's point of view. We needed to make some changes.

Lynn and I talked well into the night, and I told her about my childhood and everything afterward. She was mesmerized and understood the need for my parents and me to communicate after having been separated for so long, and uncertain as to whether or not we would ever see each other again. I understood her point of view and promised to continue my communication in a less intrusive manner. I started to call my parents before I left work. That did not sit well with them.

By April of 1981, we were happy and planning our future. Lynn asked me to marry her before I took the opportunity to ask her, and I accepted. We set an August date just two weeks prior to the day we met two years earlier. I told my parents. They liked Lynn, they respected her intelligence, but deep down, the fact that she wasn't Spanish made an impact. They couldn't communicate with her—and if they could they would be able to control her. They never understood that control is not love. Only love is love. Knowing them well, I dissuaded her from taking Spanish lessons—twice.

My father announced that he would host a dinner for our family to celebrate our wedding. I was impressed. The following week, Lynn and I, Arturo, Anita, Marta, Pepe and Carmen stood in front of my parent's apartment building, all dressed up for Arturo's special dinner.

Carmen asked, "Where are we going?"

So far it was Arturo's secret, and we were all eager to know. Arturo put his finger to his lips and said, "It's my surprise wedding gift. Special dinner is on me."

"I hope it's Tavern on the Green, Pepe said, "We'll need two taxis."

Arturo handed everyone a token and said, "We take bus." I was uncomfortable now, so I whispered to him, "What are you doing?"

"Is my obligation," he replied.

The seven of us piled onto the bus, and, by Arturo's lead, disembarked in front of the local hospital. Arturo led us in single file through the frenetic activity of the emergency room into the cafeteria.

The cafeteria was busy, noisy, filled with ambulatory patients, visitors and exhausted staff. King Arturo was in full control of his personal parade and we took our place behind him as he announced, "Tonight is meat loaf and apple pie!" He prepared trays for each of us, passed them down and told the old man behind the counter to serve seven meatloaf dinners with the works and he was going to pay. The old man double checked the line and counted us. We all raised our hands. He arranged the seven meals and served them to us one by one. Like magnets, we attached ourselves to each other and followed Arturo to the elderly woman cashier.

Arturo announced to her, "One bill, seven meatloaf dinners. I pay."

As if in a trance, we all raised our hands. She counted our hands, took Arturo's money, passed us through and like a conga line we snaked through the cafeteria, in and out of rows of tables, until Arturo found one that pleased him. "Sit!" he ordered. We complied.

There was some jockeying for the proper seating arrangement but eventually we settled in, a bit over dressed for the occasion, but Arturo was proud. I whispered to Lynn. "Your idea to elope is a good one."

CHAPTER FIFTEEN

August, 1981
The Wedding

We hosted our wedding in our two-bedroom apartment. We had an open terrace that faced the Hudson River which was filled with boats. The weather was perfect. The second bedroom was filled with catered food. Our wedding was a simple one, presided over by a female Rabbi from Lynn's synagogue. Lynn wanted to honor her father, and the Rabbi asked for his Hebrew name and included an acknowledgement as she performed the ceremony. I privately prayed to Stanley and thanked him.

We had the ceremony at noon for family and close friends, and an open house from one o'clock to six o'clock. Lynn's family from Florida flew up. The only glitch was Lynn's great aunt arriving late for the ceremony. She lived in the building a floor away and had to be called twice to appear. She believed in arriving fashionably late. Lynn was not happy.

Other than that, it was fine and fun, a wonderful mix of the people we loved. Leroy asked for permission to come dressed as Lara. Lynn and I were fine with it and s(he) seemed perfectly comfortable. Badilla and his mother and brother were in attendance. Lynn's work colleagues and her friend Richard was there. Dr. Viperman and his lesbian daughter, Tiffanie Simone attended. I would see them from time to time and we all remained friends despite the fact that I no longer attended Synagogue. They were very fond of Lynn and she of them.

My parents were quite generous and gave us cash amounting to hundreds of dollars in tens and twenties. Clearly they went through their savings and we were grateful.

Our honeymoon was short. We rented a condo in the Hamptons, a beautiful beach on Long Island. After we checked in we went to the swimming pool and rested in the sun for a while. By the time I got up to leave, my legs were severely wind burned and the skin pulled so tight, I could hardly walk. Lynn took me to the hospital; I was given medications and told to rest. But not that night, I agonizingly went down the one flight of steps to the corner phone booth to call my family. Lynn was incredulous and helped me up the flight of stairs after the call.

We went back to Manhattan after a few days. I healed well and we easily fell into a comfortable routine.

Lynn received another letter from the co-op board. After twelve years, her name came up for a parking space. She had three weeks to prove she owned a car or her name would be sent to the end of the list. I didn't know how to drive. Lynn had learned as soon as she turned eighteen, and encouraged me to learn; I did. I was thrilled when I passed the driver's test. Within the allotted time, we purchased a car. I was proud and offered to drive my parents to and from our home more than once.

"No," my father stated. "We'll crash and you'll kill us all." While in New York, he would only ride with his neighbor—unregulated, unlicensed, uninsured.

Lynn decided we were working too hard and planned fun things for us to do. She knew my parents missed me so she planned a day out for all of us. We went food shopping on Sunday morning, and as we walked through the supermarket, whatever Lynn placed in her cart, Anita removed and replaced. Lynn didn't say anything. With my parents, she couldn't do anything right. We had a quick lunch at their apartment and took the bus to the magnificent Metropolitan Museum of Art; my father still refusing to let me drive him or my mother. We truly thought my father would appreciate the objects of art, antique furniture, and the magnificent exhibits. He was bored. I asked him why.

"There's nothing to buy here," he lamented. I was hurt.

After a while, Anita decided she was tired, so instead of sitting on one of the many benches throughout the museum, she plopped herself on an exhibit.

Lynn panicked and said, "Please Mama, get up!"

Arturo took his guard post in front of Anita, folded his arms and announced, "She sit where she want!"

Too late, the alarm bells went off. From three different directions, uniformed guards circled us. A crowd gathered. Onlookers gasped and pointed. Lynn tried explaining to the guards that Anita felt faint and was unable to make it to the benches. Arturo stood defiant. I grew an ulcer on the spot. The four of us were ushered out of the museum immediately; each of us had a guard on either side. They led us down the steps to the curb. Lynn hailed the first cab she saw. The driver looked at the guards and sped off. The next cab pulled up. I pushed Anita and

Arturo into the back seat. Lynn jumped into the front seat and yelled. "Go!" The driver obeyed.

Anita and Arturo realized it was a yellow cab and thought they were being kidnapped. They started complaining. Lynn gave the driver directions while I tried to calm them down. Anita tried to hang her head out the window.

"I'll suffocate and die!" she cried.

"I no pay for taxi!" Arturo shouted in broken English. The cab driver seemed concerned by all the loud chatter. Lynn took out money and said, "Just drive!" We got them home and settled.

Lynn just didn't understand, "You can't take them anywhere."

One night in 1984, Lynn and I were having dinner and the middle finger of her right hand swelled to three times its size and turned purplish-black. She didn't think anything of it and went to work the following morning. Her boss's wife saw it, sent her immediately to her son-in-law, a doctor, and he sent her to a round of physicians over the next couple of days. By the end of the week, there was talk of removing her finger. With medication, it eventually resolved and nothing further happened.

In the meanwhile, our second bedroom was converted to a fully established business office. A work table housed various antiques. I was packing a piece for shipping one night while Lynn prepared folders and labels. She seemed tired.

"I've been asked to give another presentation at the antique club. Will you help me write it?" I asked.

"Sure," Lynn responded.

"Oh and these pieces need to be tagged and ready for shipping," I said. I heard a big sigh.

"Honey, I have early meetings tomorrow. Can't it wait?" She pleaded.

"Just two more pieces, pretty please." I pushed too hard. Lynn was angry.

"You need to make a decision to either sell shoes or sell antiques. You can't do both full-time," She said.

"I don't want to give up the union benefits," I cried.

"After so many years in the shoe business they will eventually give you two-hundred fifty dollars a month when you retire. It won't even cover breakfast," she responded.

I was feeling panicky. "What if we lose everything?"

"This is your father talking, don't become him," she warned.

"It could happen," I insisted.

"What are you really afraid of?" she asked.

"Failing and having to live with my parents again." I didn't realize how much that possibility terrified me.

"That will never, ever happen." Lynn grabbed a file and opened it. "Let me remind you of our net worth in stocks, bonds, real estate, IRA's 401Ks, savings, annuities...." I felt better about the money, but I was worried about Lynn.

Again, Lynn's forefinger swelled to triple its size and turned purplish-black. She went through the same process as the year before and again it was resolved with medication, but clearly something was developing. I called Dr. Viperman for help. He referred me to a rheumatologist.

In 1986, the co-op building's twenty-five year old mortgage was about to be paid off. Residents of all the apartments were polled to determine if they wanted to take out another mortgage or go private. Representatives of most voted to go private. The three holdouts tied up the building in litigation for seven years and eventually lost their case. Had we been able to go private in 1986, we would have had an opportunity to sell and move. We had been traveling back and forth to Florida, where I had hoped to settle and finally open a business.

Still in Manhattan, in 1986, we both changed jobs; I went to a high end department store and Lynn went to a prestigious law firm where she worked for a senior partner.

Our jobs were good, paid well and we joined a health club. Her boss eventually died of AIDS and she was transferred to another senior partner. She was slowing down a bit and it was credited to stress. She was working full time, volunteering to teach GED at night, and working with me on my small business. But she knew something was going on that was being missed by the doctors. Eventually she turned her health club membership over to me, but continued to work.

She suffered from excruciating pain cycles and high blood pressure, and was having difficulty breathing and walking, and began to use a cane. She had swellings in her brain that were getting larger and multiplying, and was told that was an indication of inflammation. At different times, almost every organ of her body was affected. With medication, she bounced back, but clearly something was amiss. The rheumatologist Dr. Viperman referred us to put her through batteries of tests. He worked with a team of doctors, which included a pulmonologist, a cardiologist, neurologist, and internist to establish a diagnosis. The side effects of the medications she was on were playing havoc with her body, and she developed ulcers and skin disorders, and had significant bone loss.

It would take nine years, but by 1993 soon after Lynn turned forty-nine, the rheumatologist, with the aid of an MRI, was able to give us a diagnosis. He was a researcher as well as a practicing physician, and was intrigued by her father's death at age forty-seven, and that of his identical twin brother at the age of thirty-nine. He was convinced there was a relationship. Lynn was diagnosed with Takayasu's Arteritis, known as a pulseless disease. It is a rare type of vasculitis, which represents a group of disorders that cause blood vessel inflammation and primarily damages the aorta—the large artery that carries blood from your heart to the rest of your body. The fear was it could cause her a stroke. That is what killed her uncle at the age of thirty-nine.

Lynn was urged to enjoy as much of her life as she could. I had never been to Las Vegas, so we planned a trip. I told my mother I was going on vacation, and she asked who I was going with. I had to remind her I was married. Some things never changed.

On the plane which stopped in Phoenix, a single woman sat next to Lynn and talked about the quality of life in the Scottsdale area of Arizona, and how she was relocating there from New York. Lynn was intrigued. Oddly enough I worked with a man who also talked about the ease of living in Scottsdale. The seeds were planted.

Our vacation in Las Vegas was fun but the best part was that Lynn walked more freely there, and felt well. On her return to New York, she reported that to the rheumatologist and he suggested she might need that dry environment.

Lynn's condition worsened and she was unable to keep up with her job, so she qualified for early retirement. She had physical therapy, and spent more time in bed. Eager to keep mentally active, she took a screenwriting course and practiced writing.

One day after a particularly difficult visit with the rheumatologist, Lynn told me how sick she was, and gave me the option to leave the marriage. The doctor had not given her a good prognosis, and let her know that things were going to get worse, much worse. Up to that point I didn't believe her illness would last, and thought surely it was temporary, and that she'd be fine. The news was sobering—there was no question, I would not leave her. How does one leave their soul mate?

By then, the co-op building was going private. Within a short time we would be able to sell and move. Reminded that her doctor suggested the west might benefit her, we planned another trip, this time back to Arizona, to Scottsdale. It was simply paradise. We even found a place for my parents and aunt. Our decision to move was solidly made. We opened an account in an

Arizona bank and secured an apartment. Lynn had it all under control.

As soon as we returned to New York, we put our apartment up for sale and within a weekend we sold it. We were on our way to Arizona. Lynn's doctors were supportive, and worked with her to settle into treatment in Scottsdale. The only concerns we had were how to tell our families?

My mother had been mugged; her gold chain stolen from around her neck which caused me to worry about their safety. We wanted them close by. My father turned eighty and was still working. I wanted to make life easier for them. Pepe and Carmen had moved out of the building long ago, but Arturo insisted on staying. The rent was cheap. The neighbors spoke Spanish.

We visited my parents and aunt more than once and sat around their kitchen table and discussed our plans to move. They refused to believe that we were moving and assumed that Lynn's disease was all in her head. Sadly, some of her family members thought the same. Since so few people had ever heard of the disease, and could not even pronounce it, they doubted it existed.

"My money stays where I can smell it," Arturo announced.

"What if there is a fire?" I asked.

"I'll have time to get it out," he responded quickly.

"It's time to manage your money so you can retire in comfort," Lynn said.

"What are they talking about?" Anita asked.

"His smart wife who thinks she's a man. Women know nothing about money. I owned two buildings...."

"Invest in real estate again, let us help you," I suggested

"Everyone wants to tear me away from my money," Arturo shot back

"What are you talking about?" I asked.

"My boss wants to send me and your mother to Spain and Hawaii for a vacation, and to oversee the new hotel chandelier installations," Arturo said off-handedly.

"That's wonderful! You should be proud." I was proud and told Lynn—she too was proud.

"Be away from my money? Are you crazy?" Arturo refused.

September 1994. Lynn and I stood atop the Empire State building and admired the view, and realized that we hadn't been there together. We were to leave in three days. After our romantic moment, we went back to my parents' apartment. We sat around the kitchen table and continued our conversation about moving to Scottsdale

"No!" Arturo pounded the table.

"What are they saying?" Anita demanded.

"I'll tell you later," Arturo responded.

"We visited senior assisted living places with full medical services," Lynn told them, I translated.

"Why should I leave this apartment?" Arturo asked.

"Because it's not safe!"

"It's cheap. No English required."

"You like going to sleep to gunshot lullabies? You'll be safe. We'll be close by. The weather is beautiful all year." I ran out of steam.

As I drove home, I watched Lynn, she was quiet.

"You have concrete wings," she said.

"What does that mean?" I asked.

"You have parents who don't move, change or grow, and you have a soul that wants to fly, to explore and to learn."

"I'm so tired of trying to please him, it's never right. It's never enough," I complained.

"Then stop! When you no longer need his approval, you'll be free to spread those beautiful wings and fly."

"So you think it's time to quit the shoe business?" I meekly asked.

"Yes! We start new in Arizona."

BOOK V

Scottsdale, Arizona

CHAPTER SIXTEEN

October, 1994
Scottsdale, Arizona

My parents continued to refuse to believe I was moving. Even after we said good-bye, they thought we would return, and so did most of Lynn's family.

We settled into a wonderful life in Scottsdale, bought our first home at the age of fifty and enjoyed the extraordinary beauty of the dessert.

The nine o'clock calls continued for a while, until Arturo put a stop to them. The phone bills were too high. After Lynn and I bought our home and settled in, Arturo and Anita realized we were not returning to New York, and made the commitment to join us in Scottsdale. Lynn made the arrangements while Arturo took charge. Lynn sent them airline tickets which could not be delivered because they removed their name from the mailbox. After several phone calls, the tickets were re-delivered and Arturo and Anita reluctantly flew out for a week's vacation. They were amazed at the cleanliness, friendliness and courtesy of everyone with whom they came in contact. They went home, packed themselves up and with Aunt Marta in tow, made plans to move to Arizona. Lynn tried making arrangements with a reputable moving company. Arturo knew a guy!

We waited for them at the airport. Their plane arrived; we waited until the last passenger disembarked. They were nowhere to be found. Lynn had an announcement broadcast in Spanish, but no response. We panicked. We located a stewardess who had flown on that flight and asked her for help.

She looked exhausted and said "I think you should sit down. I'll tell you what happened." We panicked.

She began, "A gentleman and two women entered the airplane wearing down coats with scarves and gloves. I checked their tickets twice to make sure they were on the proper flight. From the time they took their seats, the gentleman appeared to be agitated. The two women argued with each other about how to take care of him. About an hour into the flight, more than one passenger alerted me and since I speak Spanish I kept an eye on them. As best I can remember, this is how the conversation went.

Stewardess: May I help you?

Arturo: Where are you taking us?

Stewardess: Phoenix. Isn't that where you want to go?

Arturo: Too long, it's taking too long.

Stewardess: I assure you we are on time.

"The blond woman seemed agitated," the stewardess continued.

Anita: Open the window, I'm choking.

Stewardess: Perhaps if you open your coat.

"I reached over to her to help her undo her coat, but the gentleman pushed my hand away, so I reported them to the captain and asked if there was a doctor on board. Luckily there was and he accompanied me to your family. I interpreted."

Doctor: I'm a doctor, let me help you.

Arturo: No, no, there's no need.

"By this time, the blond woman moaned and appeared faint."

Doctor: Have her remove her coat for me.

"The gentleman stood in the aisle and blocked the view. The woman removed her coat and revealed a dozen gold necklaces with several sets of earrings hanging from them and gold bracelets up both arms. I understood the clothing. The doctor took her blood pressure."

Doctor: You're fine, just overdressed. Breathe slowly.

Then the doctor suggested I offer the woman a cup of water.

Anita: No drink. Have to pee-pee.

Stewardess: I'll help you to the bathroom.

Arturo: You'll have to leave the door open.

"As soon as the plane landed and the doors opened, they pushed their way out of the plane, and that's all I can tell you. You have my pity and best wishes and blessings for a good life. Now if you will excuse me, I am going to ask for a transfer!"

We were stunned. Lynn and I checked the bathrooms, had the announcement repeated, and dashed through the waiting area like lunatics. Finally, we found them sharing one cup of coffee and a croissant in a restaurant.

We herded them to the luggage area, picked up their bags and got them to the car. It was a hundred degrees outside. They were a source of curiosity as we maneuvered through the airport.

The ride home is a blank to me now. I made them as comfortable as possible, and as I helped my mother with her seatbelt my father announced he didn't need help. When I got into the front seat and looked through the mirror I noticed he had the seatbelt wrapped around his neck. Of course Anita demanded the window be opened. I turned up the air conditioner and for a few minutes all was quiet.

Seatbelts—during the many years I drove them around Scottsdale, they never mastered the seatbelts. We always left an extra ten minutes before we went anywhere just to get them belted into the car.

Lynn and I had a four-bedroom house with a pool and a fireplace. We were proud of what we accomplished and made sure everyone was comfortable in their own space. My father entered, looked at the vaulted ceiling and said, "Too big! No good."

We secured a two-bedroom, two bath apartment for them a few miles away in a good, safe area with a view of Camelback Mountain and walkable to Fashion Square Mall. As it turned out, Arturo had no credit and the only way he could get the apartment was if I guaranteed it. That did not sit well with the king. He just never understood nor took the time to learn the way business was done here.

The next day, we took them to their new doctors and pharmacies. We had a week before their furniture arrived so Lynn thought it would be nice to show them the sights.

They were only supposed to be with us one week before their furniture arrived. Remember my father knew a guy? Three months later, their furniture arrived, some of it damaged. Lynn handled all the paperwork and thankfully there was some remuneration.

Lynn's disease was advancing, and at first she approached it like a marine ready to do battle, supported by a team of traditional medical practitioners. Knowing there was no cure, she eventually focused on well-being, and was open to all methods of healing beyond traditional medicine, which made for interesting experiences for us both. She read books on healing, allopathic, homeopathic and vibrational medicine, diet and spirit.

We sought help from naturopathic doctors, physical therapists, chiropractors, psychotherapists, psychics, an angel reader, acupuncturist, numerologist, art therapist, music therapist, reiki specialist and energy specialists. She practiced Qi Gong, Yoga and deep breathing exercises. She used magnets, braces, splints and canes.

There were no support groups at the time and until twenty years later she had never met another Takayasu's patient, so there weren't people she could talk to. Thankfully, through the internet there are many groups now, although it is still a vastly unknown disease, one of the rare, invisible diseases from which people with auto-immune diseases often suffer. The New York Hospital from where she was first diagnosed now boasts a full department dedicated to vascular diseases so great progress has been made.

Lynn continued to write screenplays and I sold shoes. We worked on my part-time business and when the Internet sprang up, Lynn encouraged me to explore the opportunity of an internet business. Eventually I sold all my antiques and focused on vintage watches. With Lynn's support, I took the leap and turned my hobby into a full-time business. The internet and trade shows afforded me that opportunity, and for many years I ran a successful business.

Lynn and I were invited to a black tie event where I was to be installed as a board member of a prestigious collector's club. I sat in the middle of a dais and had a clear view of Lynn sitting in the audience, her eyes filled with pride, and locked on mine. A man spoke from the podium.

"That concludes the business portion. Now join me in welcoming our newest board member. Julian brings us his vast knowledge of antiques and collectibles, he has a successful internet business and travels extensively to the many trade shows around the country...."

As he spoke, one of the board members next to me whispered. "I wish my wife looked at me like that."

With congratulations all around, I finally was able to reach Lynn.

We embraced and she whispered, "I'm so proud of you. Remember, success isn't always based on what one becomes. Sometimes it's measured by what one overcomes."

. . .

NEW YEARS, 2000
Scottsdale, Arizona

Lynn and I hosted the party for my family; we had much to celebrate. We decorated the house. Party foods and drinks rested on table tops. The T.V. recorded the new millennium around the world.

Lynn and I were fifty-five, Arturo eighty-seven, Anita eighty-three, Marta eighty-five, Carmen seventy-seven, and Pepe eighty-two. Excitement filled the air. Lynn brought a tray of drinks to the group. Each one took a glass.

Lynn spoke, "Let's toast to Julian's retirement from the shoe business."

All but Arturo toasted me, while the others mumbled congratulations. I approached my father.

"Well, Papa, aren't you going to toast me?"

"You stupid, you gave up the union." Lynn overheard and caressed me.

"Most fathers would be proud to have their son follow in their footsteps." She kissed me.

"He'll never be as successful as me. I started sweeping the floors and ended up owning the store, the townhouse and two apartment buildings."

"And you're chauffeured to doctors and banks in a BMW," Lynn answered.

"Nobody helped me!"

Lynn answered, "This isn't about you."

"What's going on?" Anita asked.

"Why don't you two finish this in the bedroom?" Lynn said to me.

I took my father into the bedroom. We faced off.

Arturo asked, "Why did you withhold information from me?"

"You're the withholder," I responded, "you've withheld your time, your money and your love. Why don't you love me!"

"Love you? My money put food in your belly."

"You were supposed to feed me, I'm your son!"

My father answered, "I never wanted children. There's no return on the investment."

"Who takes care of you?" I responded.

"You're supposed to take care of me! I'm your father."

"Then trust me," I answered!

'Trust? I'd watch that wife of yours, tearing you away from your mother and your job. She's too smart for her own good."

"She's perfect for me. Can you trust your wife?"

"There was a time when I had my doubts. I had my lawyer make a corporation so she couldn't touch my money."

"What are you talking about?" I asked.

"I got phone calls that your mother wasn't faithful, so I confronted her, she denied it. So I said to her, 'You want a divorce, right? You take half my business?' She said no. All she wanted was you." My father belly laughed.

"That's *funny*?" I asked.

"Imagine! She didn't want my money. Yes sir, that's true love!"

"Yeah, right."

"But you knew, you little shit, and you didn't tell me."

"How could I? He would shoot you dead if I told you."

"You believed that idiot?"

"She's very convincing, especially to a five-year old."

"Ah, your mother, gorgeous, but a little scrambled eggs in the head. Know what I mean?"

"She's dyslexic," I answered, "it's a learning disability."

"You don't know what you are talking about. She's perfectly beautiful, not disabled."

"Beautiful, yes, but she made some bad decisions."

"I make all the decisions in this house."

"Maybe that's why she and Rafael...."

"Nothing but a harmless flirtation. She loves me!"

"Then why did I pray every night of my life that she wouldn't let him kill you."

"Yeah, you worried about me?"

"I still do."

"Well, I'm the king of this family, and I'm not stepping down."

Arturo walked out of the room. Anita barged in and confronted me.

"It sounds like your father is going insane. You told him, didn't you?" She said.

"Mama, I kept your secret for fifty years. But guess what? He always knew and stayed with you anyway." I left the room. Lynn embraced me and pulled me into a corner. Only she knew my pain.

"He dangles the promise of love, the one thing he knows you hope for."

"I know that now. Maybe he does love me in his own way.

"Maybe, but please don't allow him to have so much power over you."

"Not anymore, he has no more power over me."

With a new resolve, I drove my parents and aunt home. They huddled in the back seat, whispering. Because Lynn did not understand Spanish, when they whispered she knew they were either talking about her or about something they did not want her to know, so I handled all the communications. Somehow everyone was polite and got along. The incessant whispering, I couldn't cover that up anymore. On the way home it was about cutting her out of the will.

I tried unsuccessfully to convince my parents that they should plan for the future. In their minds, when it was time to go, they would simply fold their arms over their chests and die in their sleep. They agreed to have a will drawn, which was an accomplishment. We took them to an elder care attorney, a lovely lady who explained everything we needed to know in great detail. My father half listened and when she was finished asked where the real attorney (male, of course) was, and wanted to know why we had to listen to "that chubby beady-eyed girl."

I explained that she was the attorney and he had to answer some questions. He stood up and announced, "Nothing for my son, everything to my wife. That's all I have to say." The attorney was surprised given that my mother could hardly write her own name, but I took it in stride.

Within months my mother became catastrophically ill, was in and out of critical care and eventually admitted to a specialized nursing home where she was placed on a respirator. My parents were on a different medical plan than my aunt, which meant they were under the care of various doctors and had their medicines filled at separate pharmacies. This added to the time-consuming care we had to provide. My father was basically physically healthy, but was showing signs of Alzheimer's and my ninety pound aunt was down to seventy-five pounds and weakening rapidly, but remained sharp mentally.

Lynn and I took care of them full time and learned to balance the scheduled tasks and emergencies with taking varied routes so we could see new scenes, try out new restaurants, visit libraries and museums, anything to offset the anxiety and worry.

After two and a half years in the nursing home, my mother passed. Lynn wept, I cried, Marta filled her nails and my father sat mute. He had been threatening to throw himself under a bus if anything happened to my mother.

I checked on my father and my aunt constantly, and in a quiet lucent moment, my father complimented me for being a good son. Then he placed his arm around my shoulder and said," Forgive me, son. I love you."

I grabbed him tight and cried on his shoulder. He tussled my hair and kissed me on the cheek. "Go home and rest," he said.

Lynn and I worried continuously but my father and my aunt seemed to get along and protect each other. Eventually Marta required skilled nursing care and she entered a nursing home. My father needed the same and I was able to place them together. My father passed on his sixty-seventh wedding anniversary, and within a year, my aunt, having no one else to care for, passed as well.

They're all gone now, as is the pain. With Lynn by my side, all I remember is my love for them.

Beverly's Screenplays can be found at

www.burlibooks.com

- *Concrete Wings (Screenplay)*
- *Misinformed Heart*
- *Rent Money (Award winning)*
- *While I Wait*
- *Unprotected Witness*
  Co-written with Jack Knight

As well as other titles in the Burlibooks catalogue that you may enjoy.